CONTENTS

D1617291

Sophie's Story

Book 2, Sequel to Coffee, Anyone?

AMY COURTER

ISBN: 979-8-8062-9977-3

CHAPTER 1
Sophie

"Mom, this is the final and last load!" I shouted as I grabbed a box marked "toiletries" and headed for my new dorm in Willow Hall at Iowa State University. We had left my dad and my stepbrother, Jeremy, in my dorm room building a loft for me while we unloaded the truck we had borrowed from Mom's friend, Maggie.

"Wow, you guys made good time!" I said, impressed at the site of my new loft.

Jeremy said, "Yeah, I remember helping my dad put mine together a few years back, so that helped."

"It sure did, Jeremy! I couldn't have put this contraption together without you," my dad said as he gave Jeremy a huge pat on the back.

"Let me just make up your bed, Sophie, and then you will be set," my mom said, letting go of my sister Gretchen's little hand and starting for a box that said, "bedding".

"Nope. I got it, Mom. You all have helped me enough and I will be just fine." I picked up little 3-year-old Gretchen and swung her around while she cried out, "Wheeee!"

"I will miss you, sweet Gretchie, but I will be home before you know it and we will do some fun stuff when I come back home."

"Cannylan 'n O May?" Gretchen asked hopefully, her big brown eyes round as saucers.

"Yes, we will play all your favorite games when I get home and meanwhile, I will call and talk to you on the telephone, too."

Gretchen started to clap and smile until I told her, "Be good for Mom and Dad, you hear?" Her mouth turned downward, but she nodded.

We had a group hug and my parents and sister walked out the door. Then I realized; this is real. I am on my own here at ISU, I thought with trepidation.

Jeremy spoke then, "Sophie, remember, I am just a couple blocks away off campus. You have my cell number and can call me any time. You aren't alone here."

"Thanks, Jer. I really appreciate you saying that. It's kind of terrifying being on my own here, but exciting at the same time."

Jeremy laughed and said, "Yup. Freshman year is

definitely a learning experience! Don't forget you got me."

"I could never forget that!" I said hugging him goodbye.

Jeremy is my mom's biological son that she gave up for adoption when she was 18 years old. Jeremy looked her up when he turned 18. Now I can't imagine my life without him in it. He is the one who encouraged me to follow my heart when I was trying to figure out if I should call my stepmom, Amber, (Jeremy's biological mom) Mom rather than Amber. He is the best brother a girl could ask for.

Jeremy started out here at ISU four years ago majoring in animal science. He is studying to be a veterinarian and to join his dad in his practice in Storm Lake, Iowa, when he graduates. He has a couple years ahead of him yet. He is living off campus this year but not far from my dorm, and I know how to get there. It is nice knowing that I have someone in my corner, I think with a smile.

I earned a swimming scholarship to ISU, so I probably won't be spending much time in my dorm room, but I am still a little skeptical about meeting my new roommate. I have talked to Jordan through texting and facetime; we are as different as night and day, but who knows? This may work out just fine. She should be arriving tomorrow sometime because she had a "party" tonight she 2wanted to attend in her hometown of Grinnell, Iowa. At least she was fine with my dad and Jeremy building us a loft, although she said SHE wants to sleep in it.

CHAPTER 2
Amber

I feel a little lost without Sophie at home. As I think back to our tumultuous beginning, five years back when I married her dad, I thank God that we have come so far in our relationship. Sophie was just 14 and had lost her mom to a peanut allergy death the year prior, which later proved to be a murder by her mother's boss, the mayor of our town. Sophie dealt with so much in her early teen years and has grown into a beautiful, endearing soul despite the obstacles she faced along the way.

I think it may be even harder on little Gretchen, not having Sophie home. She LOVES her big sister! Gretchen has been poking around in Sophie's bedroom for over an hour now. When I went upstairs to check on her, she was sound asleep on Sophie's double bed with her thumb in her mouth. I took a pic and texted it to Sophie. Oh, yes, it will take a bit of getting used to, not having sis around.

Josh, too, has been quieter than usual when he

gets home from work. I guess we all have some adjusting to do without our sweet Sophie living with us. On that note, Josh seems to be enjoying his job with the Department of Criminal Investigation (DCI) with his home office in Fort Dodge, Iowa. It's amazing and wonderful having him home most every night for the past three years! We were able to attend Sophie's swim meets together – every one of them! We had planned outings with friends Maggie and Bob. We also attended several tennis tournaments watching Sophie's boyfriend, Bradley, compete. Gretchen was the perfect little tag-along and seemed to enjoy these outings as well!

This will be Gretchen's first year in preschool. I am still working part time at *Visitors Matter* hotel in Fort Dodge, Iowa. My good friend, Maggie took over the manager position when I took some time off the first year Gretchen was born and then went part-time. I felt I had the best of both worlds. Being able to talk with adults after a morning of gibberish, nasty diapers, and pacing the floor with a colicky baby was almost refreshing. I probably would have worked for free, although I did not tell my manager that! On the other hand, being there for Gretchen was wonderful, too, and I would not have missed that part of her early life for anything. I got to see her first tooth come in, her first step, her first word, and so many 'firsts' that I would have most likely missed had I worked full time.

My mind keeps going back to Sophie today. I know she will do great at ISU, but I'm concerned about the roommate situation. An awful roommate can make or break a freshman. I know Sophie was concerned after talking with Jordan that they were so different from each other. I am just praying that the girls will find a way to co-exist. The college doesn't like the switching of roommates until at least semester. I have faith in Sophie that she can get along with almost anybody. Besides, Sophie will be at swimming practice and swimming meets much of the time when she isn't in class, so that should make things easier as well.

Sophie's boyfriend, Bradley, opted to attend the University of Northern Iowa (UNI) with a nice tennis scholarship. It was fun to watch Sophie and Bradley's relationship blossom and grow over the four years of high school. They started out being friends the first year with an occasional group date. It is so nice knowing Bradley and Bradley's parents through our church. I can relax knowing that Bradley has a genuinely nice, stable home with loving, Christian parents. A big plus is that Bradley is absolutely smitten with little Gretchen and the relationship is mutual! Josh and I often found the three of them playing one of Gretchen's favorite board games or Hide n Go Seek, in which Sophie and Bradley usually snuck in a quick kiss or 10 pretending to ignore Gretchen's foot sticking out under the bed (her favorite place to hide) and taking their good time in finding her!

Last month Sophie taught Gretchen to swim; I caught the entire session on film! It was like a light bulb went on in Gretchen's head and suddenly, she was able to put the arms and legs together to make some movement. It was a beautiful thing! It helped that we were at the pool every single warm day since Sophie life guarded at the Rosedale Rapids Aquatic Center. The other lifeguards were gaga over Gretchen; Lindsey, Sophie's best friend, taught Gretchen to dive, so it was a group effort.

Josh and I continue to be amazed at the journey life has taken with us. When we asked Jeremy and Sophie to be Gretchen's Godparents, it was a big moment in our marriage. Jeremy is my biological son I gave up for adoption when I was 18. I knew Josh liked Jeremy (and who could NOT) but when he suggested naming Jeremy as a Godparent, I was overjoyed. I know Jeremy was also overwhelmed with our decision. Jeremy took a chance on coming to find me when he turned 18, and I am so glad he did! Our whole family has welcomed him with open arms now. He and his parents even joined us for Christmas last year! Sometimes I get choked up just looking back on my life and how God has been in it every step of the way. God is an awesome God.

CHAPTER 3
Josh

This is our new normal, not having Sophie around every day and it stinks! I really enjoyed her high school years, going to her swim meets, watching her get all dolled up for a school dance with Bradley. I think Bradley and I are on the same page since I pulled him aside way back at the beginning and told him if he dishonored Sophie in any way that there would be hell to pay with ME. Chuckling, I remember his eyes getting big and him nodding. It didn't keep him from coming back, though. Bradley is a very nice young man, and I am okay with him being in Sophie's life (since we are on the same page, that is).

I didn't think I could love a child as much as Sophie and along comes little Gretchen. What a beautiful, loving child she is! Every night when I get home from work, she runs to the door to greet me with open arms and her beautiful smile, shouting, "Daddy!" She takes after her mom with her beauty and easy-going personality. I'm so glad she loves people and loves life. I continue to struggle with that, although Amber has really helped me and prayed for me. I have to make an effort to love people and it isn't easy for me to be around a group of people. I don't like crowds--never have.

I am enjoying my position with the DCI. I still talk to my long-time buddy, Erin, at the FBI every now and then and have missed him terribly these past three years after I switched jobs. He seems to be doing okay there in Georgetown, carrying on without me. This DCI job just fell in my lap with perfect timing after a sting operation the Chief of Police, Gretchen Knoll and I put together to catch my late wife's killer, Mayor Jim Jante. Denise, my wife at the time, was having an affair with her boss, the mayor. She had wanted to leave me and marry the mayor. When she threatened to expose the affair when he refused to marry her, the mayor concocted a plan to kill Denise by using her peanut allergy as the murder weapon.

I was afraid at first that all we had was circumstantial evidence, but Mayor Jante soon dug his own grave by telling us how ingenious he was with his method of killing Denise. He bought a can of Planter's Peanuts, knowing Denise had a severe allergy to peanuts, and threw them in a half full can of Folger's coffee grounds (Denise's favorite brand of coffee) shaking it all up vigorously. He "marinated" the peanuts overnight and removed them the next day, taking the tainted can of coffee grounds back to Denise, where he knew she would make and drink coffee and die.

The mayor only admitted all this after our neighbor, Nellie Namanny, testified on the witness stand that the mayor had been "visiting" Denise several times a week and that Denise had admitted to her that she was having an affair and wanted to leave Josh and marry her boss. The last week Denise was alive she had feared the mayor because of his response to marrying her, Nellie told the jury. The mayor told Denise she would regret it if she told anyone about their arrangement. Denise told Nellie that her boss was acting scary at work, glaring at her and felt she might have pushed him too far, demanding that he leave his wife and marry her, or she would expose their relationship.

The prosecutor was able to uncover a total of 13 women that the mayor had affairs with over the years, using his position as mayor of our town to seduce them. The jury convicted the mayor unanimously. The win was bittersweet knowing that Denise wanted to leave me. Ever since, I have been attempting to be a better husband to Amber, a better dad to Sophie and little Gretchen and a better person all around. God is helping me, I know it.

I wish I could have the simple faith that Amber and Sophie have, but I struggle with giving up any control. I have been going to church with my girls and can understand why they feel comfort in going to this church. I like it too and am learning so much I didn't know before going to church there, but I am just not ready to surrender my whole self.

CHAPTER 4
Sophie

"You must be Sophie!" exclaimed a tall chubby girl I presumed to be Jordan unlocking our dormitory door where I was brushing my teeth.

I see that Jordan is a girl almost twice my size and is wearing shorts that look like they might fit me, but they definitely do NOT fit Jordan.

"Yup. And you must be Jordan!" I said, equally as enthusiastic. "How was your party last night?"

"Oh yeah, it was GOOD," said Jordan, eyeing the room and taking in my God posters. "What's up with all the religious walls here?" Jordan asked, eyes narrowing.

"I just used one wall for stuff that's important to me. You can put up what is important to you as well," I said boldly.

"Yeah. Whatever, I guess. I hope you didn't book any 8:00 AM classes. I like to sleep in and don't want the alarm going off that early."

"Well, as a matter of fact, I have ALL 8:00 AM classes, Jordan. With my schedule and swimming, they fit beautifully," I remarked.

Oh boy, we are off to an incredible beginning, I am thinking. My heart starts to sink with a sad feeling that this may be a very hard semester with each of us getting used to each other and our habits.

"I guess that's okay. I will just wear my ear plugs," said Jordan as she started to arrange her belongings. "I do hope you are not a neat freak though. Because I am NOT! At least that is what my mom tells me!"

"We'll figure it out as we go," I said, forcing friendliness in my voice. "Do you want help in making your bed?"

"Sure! Here," she said as she threw a plastic garbage sack at me. "There should be some sheets and pillows in there."

After throwing the bag at me, Jordan left the room to see what's happening on our dorm floor. Ugh, I thought, trying not to feel resentful. I offered, so I shouldn't feel resentful, right? So far, I couldn't like Jordan any LESS.

After finishing Jordan's bed making in the new loft my dad and Jeremy built, I sat down at my desk to go over my schedule and the map we were handed at orientation. It looks like I should be able to make it to all my classes in the time allowed between the classes tomorrow. I had been wondering earlier if I should have brought my bike to ride but am glad now that I didn't bring it. It would be just one more thing to keep track. I quickly put together a handwritten schedule for each day showing when I would be able to have lunch and supper each day and how much time I would have to be able to study each day. I was also determining whether or not I had time for a part-time job in there somewhere. I'm going to try a week or so and see how it goes before I commit to a job.

Jordan is back (oh YEA.) "So, are you on scholarship then, since you are an amazing, fast swimmer and all?" she asked.

"I don't know about amazing and fast, but yes, I am a swimmer and got a partial scholarship to come here and swim," I answered. "I still have to pay for room and board."

"Well, I got a full ride, including room and board," bragged Jordan. "My folks are dead broke, so that's how I got to come here free."

I wasn't sure how to answer that, since "good" or "cool" seemed inappropriate, so I said nothing.

"What are you studying?" I asked, changing the topic.

"Hopefully, very little," she laughed. Her laugh was like a hyena, and it hurt my ears. "Probably education since that seems pretty easy and you get three months off every summer."

Oh man, is she clueless or WHAT?! She obviously had her head in the sand during COVID and the struggle that our teachers went through with teaching kids. That had to be the hardest job ever. I tried not to show my shock at her answer and just said, "Ahhh," instead.

"How about you? What is your major?" Jordan asked me.

"I haven't decided for sure, but right now I am leaning toward Corporate Communications," I said.

"I don't even know what that is," said Jordan quietly. "Are you a brainiac or something?"

Not wanting to sound like a smart aleck, I said, "I am no brain surgeon, I just like to write, so I thought it might be a good fit for me."

Jordan says nothing as she lies back in her newly made bed in the loft and falls asleep for the night. She hadn't even unpacked yet.

CHAPTER 5
Josh

I rose quickly through the ranks these past three years at DCI and am now the lead investigator on many high-profile cases that include murders or missing persons.

As I step into the yellow, roped off crime scene area, it looks like this girl was a pretty, blonde teen. She has ligature marks around both hands and ankles and it appears she may have been in bondage quite a while according to the deep ligature scars. Scenes like these are so hard to observe, especially with the age and similarities of the teen girl. She could be a dead ringer for Sophie. No pun intended I sadly think. There are so many sickos out there in the world. It's very difficult to turn your daughters loose when you have seen some of the stuff I have seen.

My team discovered that the pretty teen was a missing person we have been searching for at least five weeks. Her parents had helped us put posters all over the place as well as the daily newscasts that were provided. Her name is Cynthia Coate; she worked as a lifeguard at the Furman Aquatic Center. It appears her death was by strangulation due to the deep bruising around her neck, but I'll wait for the official cause of death from our forensic guy, Gus. It also appears she was dumped in this grassy ditch after death and that she was kept somewhere else against her will those six weeks she was missing. I have a bad feeling about this, as we have not been able to find anyone that knows a reason why Cynthia would have been abducted on her way home from the Furman Aquatic Center back in July. We are still out there, though, knocking on doors and following up on any little tidbit of information brought to us. I'd sure like to find the perpetrator behind this heinous crime and put him away for a very long time.

CHAPTER 6
Sophie

My swimming coach here at ISU gave us the first morning off to get used to the campus and classes, so I don't have to swim until tonight. I pick up my school ID from my desk and head over to the cafeteria for breakfast. Jordan is still fast asleep, and her boxes are all over the place right where she dropped them last night. Hopefully she will deal with that stuff today, so I don't have to walk around it all semester!

I find my next-door neighbor, Tinsley, headed the same direction as me. "Tinsley, wait up! Are you on your way to breakfast?" I ask as I jog to catch up in the hallway.

"Yup. I didn't think anyone else besides me got stuck with 8:00's all semester! You too?"

"Yes, I have 8:00's every single day, unfortunately. They did fit nicely in my schedule, but I hate it. How about you? Just Monday-Wednesday-Fridays or every day 8:00's?" I asked.

"Just three days a week for me, a Modern Literature class I am taking," replied Tinsley.

"With Keller?" I asked hopefully.

"Yup. With Keller. Heard he's pretty good as long as you attend and participate in class," Tinsley remarked.

"Oh good!" That's the same class I'm getting up for this morning! I hadn't heard anything about him, so that's good to know," I breathed a sigh of relief.

"My older sister had him a couple of years ago and told me to take a class from him. She knows I loved my high school literature classes," Tinsley offered.

"Me too. You are from Algona, right?" I asked.

"You have a good memory!" Tinsley laughed. "Last night in the lounge when all our dorm wing had introductions was a good idea, but I've forgotten half of the girls' names already and where they are from!"

"Oh, me too, but I did remember you since you said you were majoring in Communication. That's my major, too; well, Corporate Communication is what I'm going after, but the same area of interest anyway."

"I don't remember your roommate—was she there last night?" Tinsley asked.

"No, she didn't arrive until about 9:00 PM last night. She fell asleep with her clothes on and hasn't even unpacked yet. I don't even know if she has her schedule and classes figured out. She was still asleep when I left for breakfast."

"Oh, wow. I would really hate to start out my college days like that, but to each their own, I guess," Tinsley shrugged.

Nodding, I said, "Look at this spread!" seeing the assortment of dishes we were offered for breakfast. "Scrambled eggs, boiled eggs, sausage links, hashbrowns, muffins and toast."

"Looks good, doesn't it? Hope I don't put on the 'freshman fifteen' that most college girls do!" Tinsley laughed.

"I know, right? I can eat like a horse right now, because I swim it all off in practice every day, but someday I will have to curb my eating habits I am sure," I said, adding a fruit bowl to my tray.

"Swimming, huh. What do you swim?"

"My favorite is the butterfly, but I also swim the freestyle and backstroke," I replied, picking up a glass of chocolate milk.

"Do you have swim practice every day?" Tinsley asked.

"Yes, at 6AM and again at 6PM. Sometimes on the weekends, too, depending on the relays that are scheduled."

"Oh my gosh. I won't complain about getting up

three days a week at 7AM then. You poor girl! I hope you can get your sleep every night."

"Oh, I'm okay. One good thing, swimming really helps me sleep well at night. Once I close my eyes, I'm out for the duration! I think I could sleep through a freight train whistle," I laughed.

"Let's find a place to sit and eat."

Tinsley and I went back to our dorm rooms to brush our teeth after breakfast and gather our backpacks. I noticed Jordan was STILL sleeping, although she had turned over to her back now and was snoring loudly. Shutting the door quietly, I stopped at Tinsley's door so we could walk to our first class together. "When's your next class, Tinsley?"

"Statistics at 9:00AM with McNeil. It's in the opposite corner of campus as my lit class, so I will need to hightail it out of here to be able to get there in time," Tinsley replied.

"I have Statistics next semester. My 9:00 is World History and it's not far from my lit class. I'll feel better after I have gone to all my classes and know how long I have in between them."

"Me too," Tinsley replied as we arrived at our building. "Where do you like to sit?"

"Anywhere but the front row," I laughed. We sat a few rows back but close enough to the door that

Tinsley would be able to scoot right out the door when class ended, allowing her enough time to make her 9:00 class across campus.

CHAPTER 7
Amber

I worked the other night after our new hire called in sick to work. It's hard to find good help these days. Maggie had to fire our last girl, Carrie, who worked evenings. She got caught twice sleeping on the job. Plus, she wasn't doing any of the paperwork she was to complete each night.

At *Visitors Matter* hotel tonight, a shady character came in and said, "Where's Carrie?"

I said, "Carrie no longer works here. May I help you?"

"Yeah. I guess. Need a room, cheapest you have. I like Room #101."

"Sure. Let's see. Shoot. That room is occupied tonight, sir, but the room across the hall from #101 is available. Will that work for you?"

"Shit. Okay. Carrie always saved #101 for me."

"I'm sorry we can't accommodate you, sir, but I think you will find Room #103 just as comfortable.

May I see your credit card please?"

"Carrie and I just did cash. Here is a little something extra for you," the creep winked while handing me a hundred-dollar bill.

"No, thank you, sir. I can't accept that, and I do need your credit card, please."

"Fuck, lady. I TOLD you that's not the way we do things! Didn't you fuckin' listen?! Are you stupid or something?!"

My hand went to the button under the front desk that alerted our security person of a potential problem. I pushed it twice and then said, "Sir, it's a rule here. Maybe that is why Carrie is no longer here, because all staff need to follow the rules. Now, do you have a credit card to show me or are you leaving?"

About that time, Tim, our hotel security guy, came through the lobby and said, "Hi, Amber. Everything okay?"

"Yes, Tim, thank you. This gentleman was just leaving our premises. Do you need some help, sir?" I asked the creeper.

"Bitch," he said under his breath and turned around leaving our hotel.

"Thanks, Tim, I really appreciate you coming so quickly. I was a little bit afraid of what this guy might do. NOT a nice person. Hey, when Carrie worked here, were you aware of any shady stuff going on?"

"You're welcome, Amber. Shady stuff? Like what?" Tim asked.

"Don't know. But I have a feeling some bad stuff was going on here the nights she was working."

"Well, she didn't tell me about it if she did have some stuff going on here. I was the one who caught her sleeping twice," Tim said shaking his head.

"Glad you did, Tim. We don't need someone working here that isn't doing what they are getting paid to do," I said. "Thanks again for your quick arrival."

"No problem at all, Amber. Don't hesitate to buzz me again if you need me."

"Thanks," I said, thinking about Room #101 and why the creeper might want that room. It's by the side door and has easy access from our parking lot. Bingo. "Hey, Tim, have you ever seen that creepy guy before tonight?"

"Yeah. He's been here before, but I don't know who he is. I've got his car on my video camera though. Do you want me to see if I can pick up a license plate number?" Tim asked.

"That's a great idea, Tim. Thanks!"

CHAPTER 8
Sophie

Finally, lunch time and a break until 2PM, I thought as I closed my textbook and packed up to walk back to my dorm room to dump off my backpack. Wow. Jordan must not have ANY morning classes. She is still asleep! I started walking toward the cafeteria and found a couple of other girls from my hall going that way, so we walked to lunch together. One thing I am noticing since coming to college is there does not seem to be the cliques we had in high school, where it was important to some to know what part of town you lived in, what your parents did for a living, how smart you were, etc. in order to belong to a certain group. At least for now, it seems everyone just seems to accept a person just as they are, which is great and refreshing too!

I started on one of my assignments from my morning classes when Jordan finally opened her eyes, asking, "What time is it?"

"1:20PM," I said, looking back to my assigned reading again.

"Shit. I just gaffed off my morning classes, first day," Jordan laughed.

"What all did you miss?" I asked.

"My 11:00AM and noon class, elementary reading and algebra," she said.

"Oh," I remarked, not wanting to encourage her further.

"Ah, well, there's always tomorrow, right?" She laughed as she started tossing things out of boxes looking for her shampoo and towels. "Hey, do you have $10 I can borrow? I missed lunch."

"No, sorry, I don't. I haven't figured out yet if I will have time to work or where I can fit in a part-time job, so I can't afford to spend any money right now, sorry," I said.

"It's only $10, okay? How selfish can you be, girl? I'll pay you back."

I stared at Jordan for a full five seconds and finally said, "Fine, but don't expect to be borrowing money from me on a regular basis. I simply do not have it, so I would appreciate you paying me back as soon as you can."

"Fine. Freak. Miss Tightwad. Whatever," Jordan remarked with unbelief that I was reluctant to share with her.

"Where's YOUR money, anyhow?" I asked. "Why don't you have any right now? I'm curious."

"I told you. My folks are broke," Jordan replied.

"Yeah, I remember you saying that. Didn't you work somewhere this summer to earn your own money?"

"Oh, here and there a little, but mostly I PARTIED! Woot! Woot!" Jordan shouted.

Oh boy. Guess I will have to kiss THAT $10 goodbye. All she would have had to do is get up when breakfast or lunch was being served and she could have saved MY $10! Lazy girl. I'm not liking Jordan and her mentality AT ALL. I am shaking my head thinking how this semester will likely go. Not good.

I try to study while Jordan is pawing through box after box looking for who knows what, farting the whole five minutes.

"Gotta love the beer shits!" Jordan laughs, finding her towels, shampoo, and clean clothes finally.

I decide to go to class early since I am not sure exactly where this one is. I decide to take along my assigned reading for lit and work on it while waiting for my next class. I arrive and the classroom is empty, so I pick out a seat in the second row and make myself comfortable, opening my textbook.

"Is this Speech class?" a dark-haired boy asks me as he enters the room.

"Yes, but it doesn't start until 2:00," I reply.

"Why are you here so early then?" he asked me.

"I don't know. Why are YOU here so early?" I countered.

"Oh, you are a feisty one, aren't you?" he smiled. "I'm Roy. Who are you?"

"Sophie. Nice to meet you."

"Nice to meet YOU, Sophie," he winked.

I really hate winkers. Most people who do it have ulterior motives and it's just plain creepy. I make myself half smile at him before turning back to my lit assignment.

After my afternoon classes, I walk quickly back to my dorm room, where I find a tornado has hit my room! There is not ONE SPARE SPOT to step in. Ohmygosh. What a pig. This girl cannot be human. As I try to step my way through the array of wrinkled clothes lining the floor, along with an Arby's hot ham and cheese wrapper and sack, I am asking myself if I will be able to live like this all semester. I seriously don't know. I'm not a neat freak but THIS? I don't know if I can study or even BE in this environment.

I don't want to eat a big supper before swim practice at 6:00PM so I grab an apple and yogurt at the cafeteria and take it back to my room to enjoy after swim practice, heading for the gymnasium/pool.

Wow. I think I swam faster than I have in a long time! It must be all that frustration I'm feeling from rooming with Jordan that gave me that extra bout of energy today, I think with a laugh. Walking back to my dorm room, I start talking to God and telling Him why I'm so upset with "the Jordan situation". I don't hear anything back. Nothing. But I do feel a little better just putting it all into words. Finally, back at my dorm, I kick off my shoes and see Jordan sitting on MY bed, eating an apple and a yogurt! Hold on, I say to myself. Jordan MAY have gone to the cafeteria and picked out the exact items I brought to our room about 1.5 hours ago. But, glancing toward my desk where I had put my items, mine were not there. She was eating MY apple and yogurt!! How DARE she!

"Jordan! That's my SUPPER you are eating!" I yelled.

"Really? Who eats a yogurt and apple for SUPPER? I thought it was a little snack for me since I missed supper tonight. Sorry," she said insincerely.

"Jordan, we need to talk," I said sitting down on my bed where she had put her apple core. "Seriously? Do you just place garbage EVERYWHERE?!" This is MY bed and I have to sleep here, and I don't appreciate your garbage being on it—you got that?!"

"OKAY. Chill OUT, girl. So, you ARE an OCD neat freak! My mom was afraid I would get stuck with one. She said it would serve me right."

"Jordan, I am not a neat freak, but I also don't like to walk and live in garbage. Can you do something about the mess in this room? At least keep it on your half of the room, how does that sound?"

"The mess doesn't bother me, Sophie. It sounds like it's YOUR problem. If it bothers YOU, you are welcome to clean it up," she says as she wipes her apple-yogurt-hands on my bedspread.

I actually see RED right now. I look at this girl with unbelief. How can anybody be this way? I shake my head while kicking her stuff in a pile so I can find my way to my desk. "Why did you miss supper, anyway?" I thought you would be starving since you slept through both breakfast and lunch," I said.

"Yeah, I was at the bar this afternoon just off campus for a bit and lost track of the time, so when I got to the cafeteria, they were just closing it up. I came back to our room and saw the yogurt and apple and thought, oh, how nice. My roommate thought about me missing supper and brought me a little snack."

"You were at the BAR?! What's wrong with you? Are you here to get an education or just to goof off?" I ask her incredulously. "And you had money for drinks but borrowed 10 bucks off of me?!"

"Well, I plan to goof off AND get an education hopefully. But more the goofing off part!" Jordan laughs her hyena laugh. "As far as the drinks go, I only had a couple of 'em, and they aren't free ya know."

"Well, Jordan, I don't think I am going to be able to live with you. You guilt me into borrowing my money when you had some of your own, eat my food, make a mess of our room and haven't even gone to one class yet, am I right?"

"Pretty much. But, what's it to you? Are you my mom now or something?" Jordan asks jutting out her chin.

"Jordan. I need to feel like my stuff is safe here in my room. I am paying for half this room—I guess you aren't paying for ANY of it. But, whatever, if I can't leave my stuff in my room and come back to it, I think we both need to look for different room-mates.

Jordan was silent for a while and finally said, "I'm really sorry, Sophie. I knew that yogurt and apple were yours, I admit. I was hungry, you weren't here so I ate them both. I will leave your stuff alone from now on, I promise. But the 'mess' as you call it, now that's a problem because it's the way I roll. I just don't like to waste time hanging up stuff. I much prefer piles and then I just pull out something to wear from the pile. It's kind of like a surprise each time I get dressed!" she laughs.

Despite myself, I laugh as well, saying, "Okay, Jordan. Could you at least throw the pile of clothes on your closet floor, so I am not walking on them? And garbage goes in here, the garbage can, not on a bed or floor, okay?" I am talking just like my MOM! She would probably laugh at me because I was a little pig at home. I could hardly find the floor some days due to the amount of clothes lying on it, but here at ISU with two of us living in this small room every day, it's somehow different in my opinion.

CHAPTER 9
Josh

I really hate it when Amber has to work the evening shift at *Visitors Matter*. Although she has assured me that the hotel has an excellent security guy, who is very capable. Amber called me the other night to see if I could investigate a license plate number that Tim, the hotel security guy, was able to pull off a video he had of the creep that had insulted her and tried to bribe her. Turns out this guy has been involved in several drug deals recently and a sex ring we have been trying to shut down for over a year now. We have never been able to nail him, though, due to stupid circumstances, like someone forgot to read him his Miranda rights once (because the bastard was trying to kick the crap out of the arresting officer when he started the Miranda rights process). I don't recall the other instance where he got off scott free, but I remember this guy's name. It's Tony Biggins and I'm going to be watching that creep VERY closely.

I talked to the head of FBI in Georgetown where I

worked for over 10 years before taking my current DCI role. I requested to borrow my old buddy and co-worker, Erin, who was willing to go under cover and get involved in Tony Biggins world. I was given the green light for this operation. I need to get my team together to plan how we want this operation to flow.

CHAPTER 10
Sophie

I wake up in the middle of the night to someone snoring in my ear. "Jordan! What are you doing in my bed? Get in your own bed, the loft my dad built! Jordan!"

"Whaa...t? Can't ge..up ladder," she mumbles, rolling over, smelling like beer.

Unbelievable, I think, as I get out of MY bed and crawl up the ladder to HER bed, the loft she wanted to sleep in. Looking at the clock, 2:30 AM. Ugh. Three and a half hours before I have to get up to swim. I soon drifted off until my 5:45AM alarm clock went off. I vaguely remember waking up to a snoring Jordan in my bed last night or rather, early this morning and me moving to the top loft. I dressed quickly and grabbed my suit, trudging across campus to the gym/pool thinking this day will probably be a repeat of yesterday with Jordan.

When Jordan finally wakes up about 1:30 PM, I am taking the sheets off her bed, the loft that my dad and Jeremy built. She hacks up a loogie and says, "What are you doing to my bed?"

"This is going to be MY bed now, Jordan. My dad and brother built it and I was willing to let you have it since you said you had always wanted to sleep in a loft, but since I woke up at 2:30 AM this morning with you in MY bed, I am switching with you. Get up so I can put my sheets on the loft bed."

"Hmmm. I don't remember that at all," says Jordan as she rubs the sleep from her eyes. Looking at the clock she says, "Shit. I missed lunch again. Can I borrow..."

"No, you may NOT borrow money from me again, Jordan," I interrupted. Get your head in the game. Or go back home. You are not accomplishing anything here."

"Got your message loud and clear, MOM," Jordan says with a spiteful grin. Just remember you have another bed to make when you're done with yours."

"Nope. I made yours once and didn't even get a 'thanks' for it, so this time you are flying solo, sista," I said as I fluffed a clean pillowcase on my pillow.

CHAPTER 11
Jeremy

I had a nice visit and chat with my sister at lunch today. We met at the college cafeteria and found a corner to catch up and talk. I smile as I think of Sophie's description of her new roommate, Jordan. She sounds dreadful. I doubt Jordan will even be here next semester due to her lack of ambition, so I told Sophie she probably wouldn't even have to petition for a new roommate. Jordan will most likely flunk out before semester end. I do admire Sophie's spunk when she told me about switching beds with Jordan and then her response to Jordan about borrowing money again. I chuckle as I think sometimes a person just needs to tread through some of this nasty stuff on their own. Sophie is treading beautifully. I think this experience may make her a stronger person who won't allow anyone to take advantage of her and that's okay. God never intended for us to be doormats.

I talked to Amber tonight after my part-time job at the on-campus animal clinic. She was wondering how I was and if I had seen or heard from Sophie yet. I told her very little about Sophie and my exchange since Sophie told me she didn't want to dump on her mom and dad because they might worry about her. But I did tell Amber that Sophie and I had lunch together and from what I can see, Sophie is doing awesome and not to worry.

I got to talk to my little Goddaughter, Gretchie, too. Just thinking about that kid makes me grin and laugh. She has so much personality! She will give her mom and dad a run for their money, I am positive!

I was seven or eight when my adoptive parents told me that I was adopted. I remember feeling unwanted and unloved since my "real" mom didn't want me. My parents sat me down and explained how unselfish my biological mother was in going through with the pregnancy at such a young age. They told me she had written a note that went along with the adoption. "To the Adoptive Parents: Please take good care of this baby boy and love him with all your heart. It's all I ask of you."

My parents told me that and said I was the best gift they had ever received in their lives. I still remember that day. They are the kindest, most loving parents a guy could have, and I have told myself that several times throughout my life already. And now I feel I have the best of both worlds and have two loving families.

I have been seeing a girl, Hannah, who is a senior this year at ISU studying Economics. We seem to be meshing well and have lots of common interests. I may bring her home at Thanksgiving if all goes well between now and then. But am I dating her and bringing her home for the right reason? I know it's soon expected of me to fall in love, get engaged, and marry. It is the one area of my life that I am so very confused and unsettled. If Hannah knew the 'true' me, would she like this 22-year-old virgin man? Not sure.

CHAPTER 12
Amber

I've been going through old records at work in my spare time, especially Carrie's booking of Room #101. Josh told me that the license plate number on the car that Tim had on video belongs to Tony Biggins. His name is not in our system which means that he used an alias every time he stayed here. I wonder where Tony Biggins will go for a hotel room now that Carrie isn't employed here at *Visitors Matter*. Maybe I can find out where Carrie is employed now. Maybe Tony and Carrie are in touch with each other, and he will follow her to the new hotel if she follows that line of work.

I start calling my contacts at the various hotels in Fort Dodge to see if they have Carrie Calahan employed. So far, I have called *Holiday Inn Express, Best Western Starlite Village, AmericInn, Cobblestone Inn & Suites, Baymont, Super 8, Days Inn, Sleep Inn, Quality Inn, Brookstone*, and *Country Inn & Suites*. I have forgotten how many hotels we have in Fort Dodge until I wanted to call them all. I am still waiting on two hotels to call me back since I don't have a rapport with the two that would not give me any information on their employees. I am also thinking that Carrie could be working at a Webster City or another town's hotel, if she is still with the hotel business. Tony Biggins may have a "Carrie" in lots of hotels in lots of towns, so I may be on a hunt too big for me alone. I just feel like whatever Tony Biggins and Carrie were doing, it was pure evil.

We made a new policy at *Visitors Matter* and will be keeping our videos longer than the one month we have been keeping them and taping over them. We also installed two new cameras in both our refreshment area and the front lobby by the registration desk. The cameras are very tiny and hard to spot. Tim added one more camera in the parking lot so now we have every entrance and exit covered by a camera. Tim is a gem and has been helping me with this safety project. Maggie endorsed the project after I told her what I suspected was going on when Carrie was employed in the evenings here. Tim suggested putting a camera in the two elevators, too. We have more cameras ordered.

CHAPTER 13
Josh

Erin and I put our heads together along with the rest of my DCI team. We have visited all the Fort Dodge hotels showing the staff a picture of Tony Biggins to see if he is frequenting their hotel. Tony may know he has been compromised and has a replacement while his trail cools off. My team and I feel we are in the midst of a sex trafficking ring, using our local Fort Dodge hotels until the girls can be handed off and shipped out of the area. It is just one piece to the puzzle, but if we can remove that one piece and then discover another piece, maybe we can figure out the structure and take it down. Erin is going in tonight undercover. So many times, these undercover operations do not work out and good staff end up dead. I'm praying my heart out that He can keep Erin safe, and we can stay a step ahead of these scumbags. Erin's been growing his hair out for the past month since we last talked since he knew he would be going undercover for us. I thought he looked like a "Shaggy'" but he wants to be "Squig." Ha! Go figure!

CHAPTER 14
Erin

"Who're you?" the tattooed guy demanded as he threw me up against a wall.

"It's cool, man, it's cool. I'm Squig. Pete sent me. Told me to help you guys. Call him. He'll tell you."

"Oh, I will. Don't ya worry none. Pete? Got a 'Squig' here. You know 'im? Yeah..ok."

"You're lucky I didn't blow your fuckin' head off sneakin' around here like you jest did."

"Hey, man, didn't mean ya no harm. Was just tryin' to be careful, is all. We good?" I asked, my heart almost beating out of my chest.

"Yeah, we's good. Jest don't git on my last nerve, ya got that?"

"Yip. Sure do, man," I said with huge relief. I'm in. The party is just getting started. I will listen up and learn all I can.

"What time we leavin' tonight?" a barrel-chested man asked.

"Eleven, SHARP. Don't be late," the guy with a tattooed snake around his neck answered.

"Got ya," the barrel-chested man replied.

I really wanted to say, "what's the plan?" but I'm trying not to get on the last nerve of the scary dude who threw me against the wall. My teeth have finally quit vibrating from that exchange. I'm just trying to pay attention, collect some names and figure out some stuff on my own so I don't appear too suspicious. These guys keep stuff close to the vest, so it won't be easy I know. The information is on a need-to-know basis.

It looks like the guys are all resting up and taking a snooze to get ready for whatever is going down at 11, so I do the same.

"Boss, who's the lead on this one? Want me to do it?" a low-voiced dude asked.

"Naw. I was thinkin' about havin' the new Squig guy do it, but I don't want to risk anythin' until I know more about him and what he can and can't do well. Plus, I don't quite trust him yet, ya know?"

"Yup, sure do, Boss," Low Voice said.

"I'll talk to Cam. I think he's ready. The girls will go for him, too, don't you think?" Boss asked.

"Oh yeah, Cam's a purty boy. They'll lap 'im up!" Low Voice laughed while I pretended to be taking a snooze.

I am thinking Cam is going to be the bait to lure the young girls into the dark den where they will be hauled away to another city and be used as prostitutes. I used to wonder why the girls went along with this arrangement and after I went undercover, I realized the girls have no choice. They have been made to feel dirty and ashamed and unforgiven. They are usually drugged at the beginning so that they hardly know their hand from their foot. After they have raped at least 50 times in the few days we have them enroute, they are like putty in the dirty culprit's hands. They have already cried their eyes out and have seen that nobody is going to come and save them, and they give up hope. You can see it in their eyes. It's brutal to watch. It's like their eyes lose their light and nobody is home in there anymore. I can't focus on that right now, though. I need to think about where and how this might go down and be ready for it all.

I must have dozed off for a few minutes. It's about 10:45 PM and Cam has some new threads as the boss has observed and is giving Cam the low-down of what he can and can't say to the "bitches" as he is calling them, handing him a roll of cash. We are using an old, battered van from the 90's and are starting at Walmart at their shift change to see if we can pick up any of the young help they have working there. We will chloroform her if we do, dragging her into our van and our next step will be to drop her at the hotel with Jimmy (the tattooed snake around the neck guy). She won't wake up for a couple hours or so and we should have another girl by then to add to the hotel room.

We see a slight, young blonde heading for her vehicle. We had hoped it was a girl's car that we had parked alongside, seeing the hanging objects on the mirror we were guessing it was a female vehicle. We parked between the store and her car with our sliding door able to open as soon as she gets her key out to open her car door. We were able to effortlessly snatch her up and into our van very quickly. My job this time was to chloroform her, which I reluctantly did.

Next, we drop off Cam at a crusty downtown bar and wait around the corner until he lets us know he's got one. He carries roofies to slip in girls' drinks and then "helps" take them home. It's about 1:00AM when we finally get the call to bring the van around. Cam is half carrying, half dragging a beautiful brunette out the bar door. Nobody is coming after her so that is too bad for her. It looks like we are going to get away with it. We take the beautiful brunette to the hotel as well. Two girls for a couple hours of work. I can tell the boss is pleased with himself and us as we all meet at the hotel side entrance. He has Tony Biggins with him. I haven't met him but have seen his picture online from Josh, who has been hunting for him. "Biggs", as the others are calling him, gets out of his car and tells us to unload the skank. Biggs is looking for security cameras I think and has a can of black spray paint that he squirts all over a camera near the side entrance of the hotel.

"Damn security cameras!" Biggs mumbles. "They'll be the death of us yet."

"Naw. We'll just keep movin' around so we ain't predictable. What we had with that bitch Carrie was nice, but we were prolly lucky we didn't get caught since we used the same hotel for six months," Low Voice said.

"Stop talking and help me get her ass in there," Biggs commands Low Voice.

"Yes, sir, Mr. Boss Man! Pickin' 'em up, boss, pickin' 'em up!" Low Voice chuckles.

It appears the slight blonde named Nancy from Walmart (according to her nametag) is starting to stir and wake. Biggs encourages all of us to break her in right. Bile is starting to rise in my throat thinking I will have to witness whatever goes down here. If I ever have a family, I am going to teach and train any daughter I have to be aware of all the sick schemes evil men have to capture and manipulate girls.

Nancy starts screaming when she opens her drugged eyes and sees four men standing over the bed. Biggs is ready with a cloth gag that he stuffs in her mouth, practically down her throat. She gags when she tries to scream. Tears are falling from her eyes to the mattress. I try not to watch while Biggs, Low Voice, and Cam ravage Nancy. Jimmy tells us he already broke her in. Biggs tells me I am next. I turn and say, "My ol' lady would fuckin' kill me, so thanks but no thanks."

Biggs busts out laughing, and the others join in. "No thank you, he says! Ha! Who doesn't want some free tail every now and then?! You a fuckin' faggot or something?

"Nope. Gave 'er my word man," I say, sweating now.

Biggs laughs and says, "I'll do her again for ya then."

Unfortunately, the same thing goes down with the pretty brunette about an hour or so later. Afterwards, I see Biggs taking a call outside so I pretend to need a smoke so I can eavesdrop. "Yeah, we got two tonight. Okay. See you at 4AM at Dickies."

"We pullin' up stakes?" I ask casually as I flick my cig out in the parking lot.

"In about half an hour. Take a piss and a snooze and I'll let you know when we're moving," Biggs replies.

I rack my brain trying to think where "Dickies" is. I don't know the area since I have never lived here. I need to get word to Josh somehow. Hopefully, he'll know where it is.

"Takin' a shit," I say, going into the bathroom and

locking the door.

I text Josh and tell him, "Half hour, Dickies." I then shut off my ringer.

I see a semi at an old broken-down gas station between Harcourt and Farnhamville. I can hardly make out the faded writing on the old gas station, but yes, it says, "Dickies". Hopefully, Josh knows where it is. I couldn't take the chance of waiting for his reply. I know from our conversations with the DCI team, that we don't want to interrupt the operation just yet. We want to know the complete circuit so we can take down the entire ring. I just hope we don't get lost along the way and lose the girls. To be this close and not be able to save them would be horrific.

We pull up in the van beside the semi and Biggs steps out. I can see him going over to the semi driver and stepping up to talk to him at window level. The semi driver gets out of the truck and they both head to the back of the semi, opening it wide. Biggs gets back into the van and drives over to the back of the semi where we will most likely load in the girls. They have been chloroformed again to make it easier on the semi driver I assume.

Biggs motions for us all to get out and move the girls out of the van and into the semi-truck. It looks pretty rugged back there. No blankets, no mattress, just a bare metal floor that will most likely be cold and uncomfortable when they wake up. I take the tracker Josh had given me out of my pocket and very discreetly slap it on the inside of the trailer, pretending to lose my step after laying down the pretty brunette.

"You drunk or something, Squig?" Biggs says, narrowing his eyes.

"Nope. Just lost my balance is all," I said trying to pull off a chuckle.

"Okay, everyone back in the van," Biggs says, while double tapping the back of the semi.

The semi starts to pull away and I hope and pray Josh and his guys are able to track it to the next destination.

CHAPTER 15
Sophie

Wow, the other swimmers are really, really good on the ISU team, I think as I start walking back to my dorm after evening practice. My dad made me take a bottle of pepper spray with me to college and also sign up for a self-defense course because he knew the campus walk back to my dorm from the pool was a bit of a jaunt.

I am really enjoying my self-defense course. I shake my head in wonder thinking about my teacher, a one-armed 110# woman! She was able to take me down with no problem at all. Amazing. I'll have to try my new skills out on Bradley next time I see him! I smile; I miss him. He is my best friend, (aside from Jeremy) and I can tell him anything. We've been texting madly back and forth. It's a good thing I have unlimited texting, or I'd be in trouble! Bradley is coming here next weekend and I can hardly wait!

My Jordan/roommate situation is better, I guess.

We're mostly just staying out of each other's way. Jordan actually went to a couple of classes this week--I can hardly believe it! Well, not her morning ones. I swear that girl is nocturnal. Jordan does her best work starting about 9PM at night. Sometimes she is just going to bed at 5:45AM when I am getting up to go to swim practice. I'm just thankful I sleep well every night. I don't know where she goes to study or whatever it is that she is doing, but I don't think it's in our room. She has even been waking up before the lunch line quits serving. Maybe leopards CAN change their spots or maybe "my mom talk" got to her. I chuckle as I think, I really did hear mom's voice come out of me when I was lecturing Jordan.

I suddenly am homesick for my family, all of them. I know I am a lucky girl to have the love and support at home that I have. I am also so blessed Dad found Amber and made her my mom. She is an AMAZING mom, and I am so proud to call her my mom. I hope to be just like her someday. She speaks her mind when she needs to, doesn't let anyone put her down or take her for granted. She takes care of all of us, herself included, exercising every day, eating right, getting her 7-8 hours sleep every night and drinking all her half gallon water every day. She is an amazing friend, too. She would give her friends the shirt off her back if they asked her to. I call Amber my friend as well as my mom. Oh shoot.

Sniff. Now my eyes are leaking.

I got to meet Amber's parents a couple times. Not so impressive. I thought they would be exactly like Amber. I mean, she had to learn her coolness from someone, didn't she? Well, it was quickly clear to me that Amber didn't get her personality from her mom or dad. Kind of cold fishes, both of them. Jeremy was at our house, too, that first time that Amber's parents came for dinner. I felt really bad for him. I thought they would hug him or acknowledge him as their grandson since he was blood-related, but they just nodded at him like he was nobody special. Well, Jeremy is definitely someone special to all the rest of us.

I love my dad, too. He just isn't as mushy as Mom, but I know he loves me. He is always straight forward and factual. I suppose his job has something to do with that. He has never been around much until the last three years when he switched jobs and now works in Fort Dodge. I feel like I am just getting to know him and appreciate him, since I only saw him on weekends, if that, before I was in high school.

And little Gretchie. What would I do without that little sweet soul? She even smells sweet like candy. She is so open with her love, and she gives it to everyone! She doesn't wonder or worry if someone likes her, she is just her sweet little self. And everyone DOES love her, why wouldn't they? Those adorable blonde curls and those pretty brown eyes. She is a DOLL. Gretchen's personality is so fun. She loves to play board games or pretend games and she was never really a brat. If I told her I was busy, she would go away and leave me alone. Right now, I wish I had never told her I was too busy and played with her whenever she wanted me to. She will probably be speaking long sentences by the time I see her next, I think sadly. Wow. My emotions are all over the place today. I should take a shower when I get back to my dorm and settle in for the night.

When I turn my key to open my room, I see Jordan sitting on her bed and crying with an algebra book in front of her. "Hey, what's up, Jordan?" I say non-chalantly in case she doesn't want me to know she has been crying.

Jordan sniffs and says, "Just trying to figure out Algebra II. I only took Algebra I in high school and almost flunked it, so I am taking Algebra II here and getting no credit for it since it is a required class to have been taken before I got here."

"You don't get credit for it? How does that work?" I asked.

"No, no credit. I have to pass the class, though," Jordan sighs.

I tread lightly here because I know Jordan now and know how she can take advantage of a person. But I can't help myself, "What is it you are having trouble with?"

Jordan showed me her book and I said, "Just remember, you need to do everything within parenthesis FIRST."

"Really? I must have forgotten that. I took Algebra I when I was a freshman and didn't want any part of it after that."

"You know what, Jordan? I saw on the bulletin boards by the cafeteria today that there are tutors available for every subject FREE in the Commons area every day from 9AM-11AM. You might check it out. Sometimes they can explain something so simply that it is really worth taking the time to listen."

"I didn't know that," Jordan said. "I guess I can try to get up before 9:00AM to make it over there in time. Did I tell you that I switched all my morning classes to afternoons?"

"No, I didn't know that was even possible to do," I remarked.

"Well, I had to drop a class in order to get everything else moved over to afternoons, but the class I dropped sounded boring. Anyway, I wasn't going so I probably would have flunked it, so I just dropped it."

"Okay...." I commented.

"I still have 15 hours this semester, although I am

only getting credit for 12 hours. I HAVE to keep this class, Algebra II, or the school will send me home and it's so hard for me!" Jordan cried.

"Do you know where the "Study Buddy" area is in the Commons?" I asked.

"Yes. I'll check it out tomorrow. Thanks, Sophie," Jordan said with a sniff and grimace.

"You're welcome. I hope you find someone there that's very helpful to you," I replied.

"Hey, I'm going home this weekend. There's an epic party in my hometown that EVERYBODY goes to, so you'll have the place all to yourself."

Uh oh, I'm thinking. Bradley is coming to see me this weekend and no roommate. I was going to ask one of the guys in my speech class if Bradley could stay with them so he wouldn't have to splurge for a hotel room, but maybe...he could stay with me?

CHAPTER 16
Josh

So far, so good. The tracker device I gave Erin to plant in the semi is working great and my team is able to follow it closely. We don't know how long this expedition will take. They may be taking the girls to another state. I just know we can't lose them and start all over.

As my team drives south in Missouri, I request two other vehicles for my drivers to replace the vehicles they are driving just in case the driver of the semi has noticed them following. The driver stops at a diner truck stop to get a meal and coffee. I thought about having my guys get the girls out of the truck now while the driver was in the diner, but he might check on them afterwards or feed them (although I doubt it) and then he would know we were on to him. It's better to leave the plan as we discussed earlier and try to take all the players out at the end.

The team tells me that it appears the driver is staying put for the night and has crawled up into his sleeping area of the truck. Poor girls. They have no blankets, food, mattress. Nothing according to Erin. He said he didn't even notice a pail that they could use for a bathroom. SOBs.

We have some fresh guys now watching the truck to make sure the driver doesn't get his second wind and start driving again, even though we have the tracker still showing the semi parked. I wonder if he is trying to get to the border of Mexico to unload the girls. I guess we will see soon.

I haven't been able to brief Erin on the progress, although he sends me short messages every now and again. The last one said they are going to accumulate girls until they have at least 10 of them to make it more worth everyone's while with the price of gas and all. That makes sense. I was a little surprised that they ran a semi all this way for only two girls, but I know there is a ton of money in selling these girls day after day and night after night. I bet they have found that the more girls they have in one place, the more trouble they will have in getting them in and out undetected. That may be why they took only two girls this time. DCI has authorized more agents to start following the second group of girls as soon as we get the location from Eric. We are hoping it is the same place as last time, at Dickies, but they may choose to change things up.

I am told the semi driver is awake and back in the

diner getting breakfast and coffee. Our drivers are ready for the next leg of travel. Off they all go. I can't help but be nervous that this won't go the way we need it to go. These bad asses are not stupid, and they have stayed out of jail because they are street smart. It's impossible to know every twist and turn these guys will make, especially since we don't know where they are ultimately going. We just have to hang in there a little while longer...

I arranged another trade-off of vehicles and drivers in Baton Rouge, Louisiana. The semi driver finally stoped shortly thereafter. He still hasn't opened the back of his truck to check on the girls or feed them. Maybe he is thinking they won't be his responsibility much longer. If that's the case, it's about another 10 hours to Houston, Texas from Baton Rouge. Three days is about the maximum time a person can go without water, unless he put some water in the back of the truck for them. There are so many unknowns here.

My team reported the gusty wind today and the swaying of the semi. The driver of the semi-truck is having trouble keeping the truck on the road. It just about blew over. You would think those guys would have some heavy equipment or heavy weights in the truck to keep that from happening. Those two girls hardly weigh anything. I'm hearing on my radio that the truck just flipped entirely on its side in the middle of the freeway! The truck driver is climbing out the passenger side door and is RUN-NING. Our guys following the semi-truck called it in to the local Highway Patrol in Texas, but before they did that, they got the girls out of the truck and into a transport vehicle headed back toward Iowa. The girls appear to be dehydrated and scared. We decided to pull the plug on this capture and hope the next one allows us to follow them to their final destination. I heard on the news tonight that they caught the semi driver not far from his truck and the news people said he was delusional saying, "I didn't do it. Not me. I didn't do it!" The newscasters were laughing because they said his truck was empty.

CHAPTER 17
Amber

I was on my way to Fareway this afternoon to get a few things for supper. When I got to the intersection, I had to wait for a truck before I could turn into the store parking lot. The driver of that truck was Bob—Maggie's Bob. I've been trying to figure out all afternoon why Bob would have lied to Maggie. She told me this morning she wouldn't need me at the hotel this afternoon because Bob was out of town on business, and she would work my afternoon shift so I could attend the preschool program today at 3PM. That lie coupled with who was WITH Bob is haunting me. It looked like a high school girl. Bob and Maggie's daughter, Annie, is a senior this year and if it was one of Annie's friends, I would think Annie would be with the two of them. I could be paranoid, I guess, and Bob could be innocent of any wrongdoing, but I have been in this position once before and didn't report to that friend what I witnessed only to find out years later that he had been cheating on her the entire time. Maybe I could have saved her a little grief if I had said something earlier. I feel sick. I will be the bad guy either way. If he's innocent, I'm afraid Maggie will want to shoot the messenger. If he is guilty, I'm afraid Maggie will still want to shoot the messenger. Either way, the messenger is in a bad position. I'll talk to Josh tonight and see what he recommends. Oh why, oh why, did I have to see Bob and that girl together today?

The preschool program was awesome! Josh was able to get off for an hour to attend with me but had to go back to work afterwards. I got to take Gretchen home with me after the program and she was a little chatterbox! She was the cutest one of all the little preschoolers with her little navy-blue ruffle dress! Sometimes I get teary-eyed just thinking about how much I love my girls and husband! I'm so grateful for all of them. Oh, my heart!

I made chicken enchiladas tonight with asparagus. I am very fortunate that little Gretchen is such a good little eater. She rarely turns up her nose at anything. I automatically set the table for four tonight, my mind elsewhere, then realized what I had done. I need to call Sophie soon. Her absence from our home is killing me, even though I know kids eventually leaving home for college/job/marriage is all a very normal step in life. I just need to hear her voice and then I will be okay—I think.

Josh and Gretchen loved the supper tonight and

when everyone had cleaned up their plates, I brought out my famous homemade New York cheesecake! It takes hours to make, so I started on it yesterday. I had better just have a sliver, though, since there are too many calories to even mention in this wonderful creation!

Gretchen was worn out from the preschool program and being a good girl all day. She had her bath and was in bed by 7:30 PM. I'm hoping Josh has time to brainstorm with me when I tell him about the Bob situation.

"Have you told any of this to Maggie yet?" Josh asked me.

"No," I said. "I don't want to if I don't have to. I just wanted to run it by you to see if you think I should stay out of it. But, before you answer that, I want to tell you about a time when an old friend of mine was in a similar position, and I saw her husband with another woman and said nothing. I just kept telling myself that it could be a coincidence and I should keep my suspicions to myself. Then years later, my friend found out that her husband had been cheating on her for years and she felt she wasted so much time with him while he was busy being such a cheat and liar. I have regretted not telling her what I saw ever since."

"Ahh. So, I need to factor that in along with what you just told me about seeing Bob with the high school girl, right?" Josh asked.

"Yes, because I don't want to make that mistake again."

Josh said, "I know a guy who owes me a favor. Would you want me to have him follow Bob around for a week or so to see what's going on with him?"

"Yes! Then nobody would have to know if there is a legitimate reason why Bob and this young girl were together. I can't imagine what that reason would be, but there could be one, right?"

Josh shrugs and said, "I guess, but like you, I can't imagine what it would be."

"Okay. It's settled then. Have your guy follow Bob and his truck around for a bit and we will see what shakes loose. I have Bob's license plate in my purse for you because Maggie loaned me Bob's truck when we took Sophie to ISU."

"Good. That will help," said Josh.

"Where are you with Erin's undercover journey? If you can tell me, that is."

Josh sighed and said, "We have to start over again. The semi-driver that had the girls in order to deliver them had an accident and rolled the truck near the Louisiana and Texas border, so we stepped in and rescued the girls when the trucker ran off. He didn't get far, though, and is in custody now. The police force in Louisiana thinks he is crazy because he was talking about how he had nothing to do with the girls and the truck was empty so probably no charge will stick since they can't prove anything."

"Why didn't you just leave the girls in the truck to be found so you could get the trucker arrested?" I asked.

"We had to make a quick decision when it happened, and we felt that a rescue was what we should do. When we rescued the girls, we took our tracker out of the truck so authorities would not find it. Part of that decision being made was that we were hoping the sex ring wasn't aware of any observation and continues like usual so we can catch them in the act again, but closer to the destination so we can get all the guys involved and lock them up."

"Erin will be staying in place undercover then for the time being, right?" I ask.

"Yes, unfortunately. I really want to get him out of the undercover fiasco as soon as possible, but I am afraid we really do need him on the inside so we can figure out who all the players are and the pickup and drop-off locations. It would be impossible to establish this without Erin. I just hope we can keep him safe while we figure all this out."

"Amen," I said.

CHAPTER 18
Sophie

"You're here!!" I cried as I jumped into Bradley's arms in the Visitor's Parking Area on campus.

"Finally!! It's been TOO long without you!" Bradley smiles, kissing me enthusiastically. "Wow. I couldn't believe how far away from your dorm I had to park," Bradley said.

"I know. That's why I didn't bring a car to campus. That and the fact that I don't really HAVE a car," I chuckled. "Otherwise, I would be way out here in the boonies and what good does that do me to have a car parked way out here?"

"Right," Bradley said as he pulled his bag from the trunk. "Where am I staying? Did you talk to someone in your speech class yet?"

"About that," I paused looking away from Bradley. "My roommate is gone for the weekend, so I just thought you might as well stay with me in my room." I could feel my face turning red even as I said it.

"Really," Bradley says, narrowing his eyes at me. "We can hardly keep our hands off each other when people are in our midst. How do you think we'll be able to keep anything from happening if we have a closed, locked door?"

I looked at my shoes and said, "Maybe we shouldn't worry about that." Again, I can feel my face heating up.

Bradley starts to laugh and says, "We can figure that out later. Show me your room, the campus, the pool, everything! Oh shoot! I won't be able to meet your charming roommate, will I?"

"Nope. Not this time. Jordan had an important PAR-TAY she needed to attend in Grinnell, her home-town. She's the reason we have an empty room," I said with an arched eyebrow and smile.

"Thank you, Ms. Jordan!" Josh laughs. "You really got the pick of the litter, didn't you, as far as room-mates go?"

"The first week was the roughest with Jordan. Then I gave her 'my mom talk' and believe it or not, it kind of sunk in! I suggested earlier this week that she start going to the free tutoring sessions offered by the college and she thought she might do that. Of course, the tutoring sessions are in the morn-ings and that is when Jordan does her best sleeping, so I'm not holding my breath!"

"Yeah, I wouldn't either! Hey, at UNI they just

started an evening session of tutoring since that is when a lot of the students end up studying. We have one from 7-9PM that I am helping with. That's when I get some of my own studying done right now. I think the attendance will pick up, though, when the students realize there is help now in the evenings as well as the mornings."

"Huh. That's a good idea. I wonder if ISU would also adopt that. I need a part-time job as well. I may talk to my advisor to see who I need to talk to in order to suggest it."

"Good for you. Just hope that you don't get Jordan as your student!" Bradley laughs.

"Oh! Good point! Maybe I should wait until next semester to suggest it!"

I show Bradley everything on ISU campus; all the fun places: the bike path, the pool I swim in twice a day, my room, the Simon Estes Music Hall, and the Communication Building where I attend several of my classes. We end up at Memorial Union, where I treat Bradley to a frappe caramel iced coffee. "Oh, my brother, Jeremy, invited us to his apartment for supper tonight! He's making spaghetti and meatballs and garlic bread!"

"Sounds great! I have worked up an appetite with all this walking! Hey, didn't you say you could get to all your classes without being late? How do you do that? They only give you 10 minutes, don't they?"

"Yes. I do have to jog between two of the classes that are on opposite ends of campus. Not sure what I am going to do when it snows or is icy. Maybe put some snowshoes on my boots, what do you think?"

"Only if it is downhill to the second class!" Bradley laughed.

"I guess I will cross that bridge when I get there," I say. "Let's get a move on to Jeremy's place. Do you need anything from the room before we take off?"

"Nope, just you, babe! I have missed you so much! I didn't realize how often you were in my everyday life until I no longer HAVE you in my everyday life!" Bradley said.

"I know exactly what you mean, Bradley, but I love all the texts we send back and forth. I feel like you are kind of with me on campus when I text and walk. Except the jaunt between my two furthest classes; I do NOT text you while running!"

"That's good. Mind on task, right?"

"Right. We're here! This apartment is Jeremy's. He is looking for a roommate. The roommate he had lined up ended up switching colleges at the last minute because he got a better scholarship at the University of Iowa. Jeremy had already signed the lease, so he is pretty much stuck unless he can find a roommate. He's working some extra hours to try to pay for the whole apartment."

"Wow. That's rough," Bradley said.

"Welcome, you two! Bradley, good to see you again! I knew you couldn't stay away from this girl for very long!" Jeremy said.

"Nope. I sure am glad to get to visit. We planned this before either of us even got to our separate campuses!" Bradley said.

Jeremy said, "Now why doesn't that surprise me?"

"How's it going, Sophie? Any more good roommate stories?" Jeremy asked.

"No, fresh out of them! But the situation is a little better. Not perfect, but a little better."

"That's good. You guys hungry, I hope?" Jeremy asked.

"You bet!" Bradley and I say in unison.

"Bradley and Sophie, this is Hannah. Hannah—Bradley and Sophie," introduces Jeremy.

"About time we get to meet, Hannah! I have heard a lot about you!" I spoke.

"And I have heard a lot about you as well, Sophie!" Hannah said as she smiled.

"I'm with her," Bradley says pointing at me. "Boyfriend."

Laughing, Hannah said, "So I gathered! Nice to meet you as well, Bradley."

"Now that we have that out of the way, let's EAT!" Jeremy said.

It was DELISH! It was just like other times when Jeremy would come over to the house and eat with our family and Bradley. We never run out of things to talk about. Jeremy is a pretty good cook, too. I could learn a thing or two from him, I think with a smile. Bradley and I help with the dishes, me washing, Bradley drying, and Jeremy is putting everything back in its proper place with the help of Hannah.

"Leftovers! I love leftovers!" Jeremy said after slipping the last container back in the refrigerator for another day. He wiggles his eyebrows at Hannah.

"Does that mean I'm invited over tomorrow to finish them?" Hannah asked.

"Always!" Jeremy said with a smile.

"Glad we didn't eat you out of house and home, then, Jeremy," Bradley replies.

"Thanks so much for supper, Jeremy. You are the BEST," I say with a hug for my brother. "It was great finally meeting you, Hannah!"

"Yes," said Bradley. "Nice to meet you, Hannah."

"The pleasure was mine," said Hannah.

Jeremy and Bradley shake hands with a shoulder hug because I guess that's how 'bros' do it. "You are welcome! See you around soon, I am sure, Bradley," Jeremy replies. "And see you, Sophie, Tuesday night.

I'm coming to your first swimming meet since it is here."

"Awww, thanks, Jeremy! Mom and Dad won't be able to come so that's really cool! I appreciate it!"

"Wouldn't miss it for the world!" Jeremy said as Bradley and I start on our walk back to the dorm.

"That was fun," Bradley said quietly.

"Yes, it was. Jeremy is the best big brother any girl could wish for. I liked Hannah, too. And I am such a lucky girl to have such a handsome, studly boyfriend! I could not have picked out a better boyfriend if I had custom-designed him myself!"

"Flattery will get you everywhere!" Bradley says with a smile. "And back at you, Sophie. I love you."

"I love you, too, Bradley."

As we enter my dorm, I say, "I don't have a TV in my room, but there is one at the end of the hall if you want to watch TV."

"Nah. I can watch TV any time, but I don't get to see you every day. There's something I have been thinking about that I want to ask you."

"What is it, Bradley?"

Bradley closes my dorm room door and slowly drops to one knee, digging in his pocket. I am so stunned I can't even swallow. "Wh....Brad..."

"Sophie, I know we have talked about this and

wanted to do this down the road, but can we make it official? Will you marry me?"

I pull the ring out of the box and turn it over and see the inscription inside, 'Promised Love'.

"Oh, Bradley, it's beautiful! YES!" I yelled, throwing my arms around him and kissing him passionately.

When we finally unfold from one another, I asked, "What made you jump-start our plan?"

"I think by being apart—us each going to separate colleges, just made me realize how much I love and miss you and I wanted to make you mine! I thought about waiting until Christmas, but I couldn't even wait that long to hear you give me your answer."

"You knew what my answer would be though, right?" I asked incredulously.

"Yes, I was 99.9% sure I did, but I still have been a nervous wreck," he smiled sheepishly. "We've talked about this since last year when we were seniors in high school and established our plan to marry the minute we each graduated. You still want to wait that long, Sophie?"

"Do we have a choice, Bradley?" I asked confused.

"We always have a choice, Sophie."

"What are you thinking, then?" I asked.

"How about if you look into transferring to UNI next fall? We could get married either this summer or even spring if you want?"

"I don't know, Bradley. I checked out scholarships at UNI when I found you were going there, but they wouldn't give me much. Don't get me wrong—I want to marry you. I just don't know about the timing and transferring to UNI."

"Well, we have some time to figure it all out. Just be thinking how we can make this work. I do know that there are transfer scholarships as well and maybe you wouldn't even have to swim for your scholarship—just take the transfer scholarship. And if we are married, we might get a 'poor folk' scholarship since it would be your income and mine combined."

"Wow. You have given me a lot to think about, Bradley. I definitely will look into this. How exciting! We're going to get MARRIED!!!" I danced. "Can you climb ladders? Because my bed is up there in that cool loft you made, and I want to make out with you on my bed rather than Jordan's."

"Uh...okay—you don't have to ask me twice!" Bradley said while slipping off his shoes and scrambling up the ladder.

Sometime later I hear my cell phone ring. My mom's ringtone. It's probably good timing, although I don't want it to be. I look down on the floor under my loft and see my jeans down there, along with my cell. I look at Bradley and he nods that I should answer it. I climb down in my underwear and bra and answer, "Hi, Mom."

Mom will never know how timely her call was. Both Bradley and I really want to wait until we are married to have sex. It just seems so impossible sometimes. But now that we have moved up the wedding, I think we can manage to wait a little bit longer for sex. Now that I'm not lying on my bed in his arms, that is. Bradley kisses SO GOOD!

"Close call." Bradley says as he climbs down and puts on his jeans after I hang up from my mom's call. "How did these clothes get off us, anyway?" he asked with his sexy grin.

"I know, right?! They just kind of FELL off us. I don't remember taking anything off."

"That's because I took yours off and you took mine off," Bradley snorted.

"Oh, right. That makes sense," I laughed.

"You didn't tell your mom our news," Bradley said.

"No, we hadn't talked about announcing it yet, so I thought I would wait to see how we want to do that. How DO you want to do that?"

"Do you want to wait until Christmas to announce it?" Bradley asked.

"I think we need to come up with a date before we announce it because you KNOW that will be the first question after announcing our engagement."

Bradley laughs, "Right. Actually, I did look into how far ahead you need a marriage license; it's 72 hours before the wedding. The marriage license expires 30-90 days later, depending on circumstances, so there isn't that much of a window."

"That's good to keep in mind. We need to know at least 9 days ahead of time. We can do that, right?!" I laughed.

"Let's just think about this for a while before we announce it and check out some stuff. I will investigate married housing on UNI campus and transfer scholarships. You check out how many of your credits will transfer over to UNI. Hopefully, all of them will, but at least next semester, you can choose classes that definitely transfer over."

"Sounds like a good plan. Or we could see how YOU could transfer to ISU? It would be a lot less complicated for me!" I say seriously.

"Hmm. I hadn't thought of going that direction, but let's check that out as well." We have to think about what is cheaper in the long run for both of us combined since they are both good schools."

"Good. We will keep our minds open to either possibility then," I say as I kiss my guy good.

CHAPTER 19
Josh

I feel defeated this morning. Defeated that we were not able to see that first maneuver through to the end and catch the two girls' creeps red handed, and defeated that I don't feel in control of anything. This is when I am most vulnerable and tempted with my secret vice: gambling.

I wish it wasn't quite so easy. All I need to do is open my laptop and there it is. Begging me to click, sucking me right in. I've never told Amber the truth about my gambling problem and luckily last year I was able to win back a substantial amount after losing an even MORE substantial amount. I don't know why I do it, truthfully, except it makes me feel better for a short period of time but then worse than ever afterwards. I use a secret account that I had started several years ago for a vehicle for Sophie, so now she has no vehicle. She was able to borrow ours in high school whenever she needed to get somewhere, but I was going to present her with a nice used car for her to take to college. When I lost most of the money in the account last year, I couldn't do it and of course, sweet Sophie said she really didn't need a vehicle anyway—that it would just be in the way. I'm ashamed of myself. Yet, I want what I want.

It looks like my dreaded addiction to gambling will have to wait; Erin just texted me that the team has been collecting girls all week. The goal is to get enough of them to fill the truck. They are hoping for 20 girls by Sunday morning for transport. I need to round up some more of my team for this weekend.

I've been thinking about the conversation with my private investigator this morning that I told Amber owed me a favor. Conner has been following Bob and taken some very compromising photographs of Bob and the girl this week already. He has a female contact in place to befriend the girl Bob had in his truck. Amber thought the girl was still in high school, but the girl actually just graduated last year and is 19 years old and works as a waitress at Applebees. Bob is 42 and yes, they are having an affair. I was really hoping there was an explanation for Bob being with the young girl. What a shit. He has a daughter one year younger than the girl he is having an affair with; what the hell is wrong with him? And to think that he had both Amber and me so conned when we had supper with Maggie and him. We thought Bob was a good guy. I certainly don't think that anymore--he's been bluffing the whole time. Now I have to let Amber know and she has to figure out what she will do with this information. I don't envy her one bit. Maggie and Annie will be devastated with the actions of Bluffing bullshit Bob.

I was amazed to find out that you can play poker, blackjack, slots, and even scratch lottery tickets online without even leaving your home or office. Of course, you have to make sure you're going to the right legal gambling sites; there are so many crooks out there that have made their own gambling websites and try to suck you in. It's just way too easy to gamble these days. I don't even have to go to the casino. I love lottery tickets, card games, the horses and even the dog races and I can do it all with a couple of strokes on my keyboard and nobody ever knows what I have been up to, until I lose big, that is.

I read somewhere that the odds of winning scratch tickets are 1:4.3. That means that out of every 43 tickets sold, about 10 will get a prize. So, 3 out of 4 tickets have no prizes. Those aren't very good odds and I have never been a particularly lucky guy, so again, why do I do this? I ask myself this all the time but when I finally win something over $50, I say to myself, "THIS is why I do it!" I guess it's the thrill of the win that keeps me betting. Last year when I got in the hole so deep, I even thought about calling the gambling phone line that is advertised, but then I started winning back some of my losses, so I shut that idea down quickly.

Last year when I got into some serious debt, I was playing poker online, so I have at least quit doing that. It was MUCH too easy to drop $500-$1,000 a day. I did win some back after losing a bunch, but then it was harder to quit when my luck was good, hoping I'd win back all that I lost. I've always thought that I'm not hurting anybody with this secret vice, but after thinking about Bluffing bullshit Bob and his deceit, maybe I'm not so sure. Maybe I'm no better because I'm lying too. Amber, Sophie, and Gretchen don't deserve this.

I sigh as I click on a roll of 300 scratch tickets and start scratching them online. I've just spent $600 of our hard-earned cash. I'm an addict.

CHAPTER 20
Maggie

I had to get out of there and took the afternoon as a sick day. It's the dang truth—I feel SICK. When Amber told me what she did about Bob, I was sure she was mistaken. Bob couldn't and wouldn't do that to Annie and me; I was positive. But then I started accumulating all the half-truths I felt Bob had been telling me for quite some time that didn't quite make sense to me, like a fuel bill from a Caseys in another town or the time we were charged for a hotel stay several months ago and he said it was a mistake and he would call and get it taken off our credit card.

Bob and I were high school sweethearts and have been together forever; almost 20 years now! I've never been with anyone else and haven't even given a thought to being with anyone else. It's just always been Bob and Maggie. Maggie and Bob.

Amber even had some pictures to support her suspicions. I feel so stupid. How could I not know this was going on? Right. Under. My. Nose. I guess I am too naïve and trusting. When Bob told me he was going to the gym to work out, I believed him. I do remember once, though, a couple weeks ago when he came home from the gym (or so he said) and I opened his gym bag to wash what was in there. His workout clothes were neatly folded and unused. He obviously had NOT been to the gym. When I asked him about it, he just laughed and said he got talked out of it by some of the guys from work who were going for beers. I am just wondering how long this has been going on. It makes me sick to think about. It also makes me think what diseases I could have caught from him being unfaithful.

A few months ago, Bob started going to the gym a lot more frequently and dropped some weight or redistributed it to muscle, and he got very ripped. I remember telling him how sexy he looked. I wondered if that was the point when all this started or was it before then when he said his paycheck was smaller because of some new tax law and I needed to find a job that paid better. We couldn't even pay our house payment that month. I had to call the bank and work out a new payment plan. Was the affair going on back then when this girl would have been 18 years old?! Or was it another girl altogether? This is killing me. I need to confront Bob and get to the core of this. After texting Bob to make sure he was going to be coming home tonight for supper, I called Amber and asked her if she could call and ask Annie to babysit Gretchen tonight so I could have the house alone with Bob.

***

Oh, this is rich; it's really rich. Bob said he hasn't been happy for over 20 years and that I have changed. He said ever since I had Annie, 17 years ago I haven't given him the time of day. He said I pushed him away and didn't wanted sex when Annie was little and so he found it elsewhere, starting way back then. Well, yeah, when you get up in the middle of the night with a teething 2-year-old for several hours and still have to get up to go to your full-time job while your man gets his full 8-hour night's sleep, it's a little hard to feel up for sex. We've had conversations over the years about the fairness of our divided chores. Bob has always felt I should do more than him around the house since my paycheck isn't as high as his from his trucking job. Basically, Bob wants to do nothing around the house and leaves the bill paying, dishes, grocery shopping, cleaning, and lawn mowing to me. At the beginning Bob said he would cook, but I sure haven't seen much of that for quite some time.

Then there are the toys Bob just had to have. The expensive guitars he "tries" to play and sing with, the golf clubs and memberships, the expensive trips to Colorado snowboarding every year with buddies, the boat. I could go on and on. I try to think of my toys and all I can come up with is my new vacuum sweeper that Bob had a fit about because it was so expensive. I guess that is MY "toy".

I patiently listened while Bob went on and on about why he isn't happy and hasn't been for quite some time. When he was finished, I asked him if he wanted to go to counseling with me to try to save our marriage or if he wanted a divorce. Well, he has a little honey and wants a divorce. He admitted to having numerous affairs over the years. I think what hurt me the most was when he told me that he was with different girls when we were in college engaged to be married! Why did he ask me to marry him if he still wanted to mess around? I don't understand him at all. I feel like I have wasted 20 years with this man I don't even know.

CHAPTER 21
Sophie

I'm so excited! I finally found some part-time work that won't take a lot of my time but will help with some of my expenses. I talked to my advisor last week hoping I could find something in my field of communications that could benefit me dollar wise as well as some good experience. She tasked me with organizing and running the Blood Drive on campus in two weeks. My advisor said I can do anything I want to get the students there. I am jotting down some notes as ideas strike me. First, I will put together some posters and put them up in all the lunchrooms and lounges at ISU, maybe even the bathrooms, too, I think, as I jot that down as well. Next, I will put something on our school network to all the students about giving blood and the benefits. What else? I need some unique idea that is not usually done here to capture the attention of my classmates...I know! People always want a little something when they give a little something. I'll call around to the local businesses to see if they will donate a $40 prize to the cause and we can have a drawing of all the students that participate! I better get busy!

As I'm waiting for the manager of Arnold's Motor Supply to pick up the line, I'm thinking about Jordan and some changes in her. She has been setting her alarm and getting up for those free tutoring sessions for her algebra class. I was amazed when she told me she made it to several sessions last week and they were really helping her. Jordan even thanked me for telling her about them and told me she got a D on this last test and was so excited since she failed the first one. I told her I was happy if she was happy! She's also been keeping her unbelievable pile of loose clothes on the floor of her closet instead of on our floor in the room. I'm really glad Jordan and I are different sizes so she doesn't try to borrow my clothes. I seriously do not know how she tells if her clothes are clean or not, because I just see her throw them back into the pile when she takes them off. Oh well, as long as our room doesn't start stinking..

"Hello, this is Jay, the Manager. How can I help you?"

"Hi, Sir, this is Sophie Jackson, a student at ISU. I have been tasked with the ISU campus blood drive this year and would like to have an incentive to entice the students into giving blood. I am wondering if you can help me with that and donate a $40 prize from your business that we could use for a drawing of the blood donor participants?"

"Sure, why not?" Jay said. "Will you be picking up the prize or how do you want to do this?"

"Thank you so much, Jay! That is awesome! Actually, I would like the student to come to you and pick up his/her prize. I'm a freshman and don't have a vehicle so I am wondering if you would take a selfie of you and the prize along with the ISU blood donor winner and send it to me. I will be collecting and sending the pictures of all the participating businesses, prizes, and blood donor winners of the drawing to our local paper and also our campus paper for recognition."

"Hey, not bad, Sophie Jackson! I really like your idea. I have been wanting to do some advertising for Arnold's Motor Supply and this will be a place to start. Advertising for only a $40 item donated! Not a bad deal at all!"

"That's great to hear! Thank you. What is your email there at Arnolds Motor Supply? I will email you so that you will have my email address and then you can message me what you plan to donate so I can put that in my advertising for the event?"

"You have really thought this out and it's a very good plan, I must add. My email address is: jay@arnoldsmtrsply.net. I'll look through my inventory and email you later today with the prize I plan to donate."

"Thanks again, Jay, and talk to you soon!"

I'm off to a good start with my first call. I just hope all the businesses I call are as receptive as Jay from Arnolds Motor Supply. If this all works out as I plan, I have another idea to run by my advisor.

I also talked to my advisor about Bradley and my plan to get married this spring or summer. I asked her if she had time to help me with seeing what classes at ISU that I have taken would transfer to UNI. She didn't have time today but gave me a pamphlet of which classes were interchangeable at both schools and told me I needed to talk to the Transfer Admissions Office as well. That's next on my agenda.

I found out that I can get a $1,000 transfer scholarship to UNI if I have at least a 3.0 GPA and maintain it for the year. I can renew the $1,000 scholarship each year after that if I maintain the 3.0 GPA. That's not a lot but I have factored in the amount of time I spend swimming each day that I could be working and earning money on campus and found I would actually be ahead in dollars if I gave up my swimming scholarship and just worked at UNI, provided I can find a job on campus, since I don't own a vehicle.

I googled married housing at ISU and found out that married housing on campus is $56/month + utilities! The campus is in the process of building new married housing units. But, on the downside, only half of the married students are allowed to live in these units on campus. I don't know what the criteria of the lucky half is. I wonder what Bradley has found out on his end.

I just had an incredible thought! What if Bradley and I get married this summer and he transfers his classes to ISU, and we could live in the same apartment as Jeremy and share expenses with him! We could take turns cooking and share grocery bills three ways. I wonder if Bradley will go for this?!

CHAPTER 22
Jeremy

Sophie swam great at the swim meet last week, but I can tell she doesn't like not winning first place in her events like she was used to doing in high school. I told her that they took the best from all the high schools and that is who she is competing against now and to hang in there. I could tell something was on Sophie's mind the other night when we got together. She told me about Bradley and his proposal and his idea of moving up the wedding. She wasn't as excited about the idea Bradley had of her transferring to UNI. I thought it was because of the swimming but she told me it was because of me. That blessed my heart, sweet Sophie.

I've been thinking more about my relationship with Hannah. She is a beautiful, smart girl, but I just don't know if the chemistry is there. I'm not sure I love her. She's not a Sophie. It's a good thing I didn't make Hannah the offer already to take her home at Thanksgiving because I am second guessing myself on that right now. I can't help feeling like there may be something wrong with me. Why don't I love Hannah? I should, right? I mean, why would I NOT love Hannah? I have been trying to sort it out for a while now. I am not attracted to guys, so I am definitely not gay. Maybe I just haven't met the right one yet. I think I am comparing the girls I meet to Sophie and Hannah is not a Sophie. I probably should let Hannah go so she can find the right person for her.

I will really hate to have Sophie transfer to UNI, but I totally get why she and Bradley want to be at the same university. I will miss her like crazy, but I will still be able to see her from time to time at family stuff since Amber and Josh have started including my mom and dad in their family gatherings, along with me. Maybe Sophie can convince Bradley to come to ISU instead. I really liked her idea of the three of us living together in my apartment. I'll have more free time to work if Hannah and I aren't together anymore, so I can probably hang on to paying rent by myself for a while longer until Sophie and Bradley figure out what they are going to do. It will be interesting to see what those two come up with.

CHAPTER 23
Amber

I feel so bad for Maggie. I can tell how much pain she is in by just looking at her eyes and the dark circles under them. Bob has moved out and they have now agreed to file for divorce. I told her about a really good lawyer she should get in order to take Bob to the cleaners. I told her she needs to get everything in writing, not just agree with a handshake or whatever. I told her to remember Bob LIES, so she needs to get everything legalized so she and Annie can get what is coming to them. Bob quit college his freshman year due to his lack of ambition and his lazy butt. After Maggie graduated, they got married and Maggie helped pay off Bob's student loan along with her own, as well as his car loan. The dirt-ball. I hate what he has done to Maggie.

Maggie told me she went to the doctor to get tested for any STD she may have contracted from Bob. I was hoping she had a clean bill of health so as not to give her any additional stress from Bob and what he has put her through, but after the testing, Maggie found out she has gonorrhea. She called Bob to tell him so he could "do the right thing" and let his sexual partners know that he possibly gave them a STD, and he had the nerve to tell Maggie that she didn't get it from HIM! He is ridiculous. So, he will just keep spreading the STD around. Maggie is getting treated with an antibiotic right now. Poor Maggie, although she's lucky the STD is a curable one and not a permanent one.

I asked her how Annie was doing, and Maggie said she has friends in similar circumstances, so she thinks she is able to talk to them. I had been worried about Annie and her self-harm a few years back and Maggie said she hasn't seen any evidence of that again, so hopefully, dirt-ball Bob hasn't reopened that old tendency of Annie's.

When Annie was 12, she started to self-harm by cutting herself. She had everything going for her—she was cute, funny, had a darling figure and was well liked. Nobody could figure out why she was self-harming. Maggie set Annie up with a therapist who was able to help as well as our church youth group. After some therapy and lots of prayers, Annie later admitted she didn't really know why she self-harmed, but that it could have been a coping mechanism, exchanging one pain for another. I'm just hoping the pain of this divorce isn't too much for her.

Meanwhile, it appears Bob has squirreled away a

sizeable amount of money and has put a down payment on another house in town for him and his little 19-year-old honey. It's pretty comical; last week Maggie asked him to split the cost of college tuition for Annie next fall with her and he said he was just too broke. He makes me sick. What a lying piece of crap Bob is, or as Josh likes to refer to him as, Bluffing bullshit Bob.

CHAPTER 24
Josh

Erin tells me to be ready for the exchange. They "stacked" the girls in the van after chloroforming them and are on the move to the same drop off at Dickies. They are meeting the semi driver at 3AM in the morning. I've got my crew ready to move at a moment's notice. We even put up a couple small undetectable cameras in the area today.

Erin and his people are right on time, and we can see from the camera view most of the exchange. I can hardly believe how they are tossing those girls in the semi like pieces of frozen meat. One guy has the legs and one the arms and they just swing them into the truck. I counted and just like Erin said, there are 20 girls knocked out, drugged, and zip tied. Before they closed and locked the semi, Erin was able to slap another tracker on the inside of the semi just like last time. Our drivers start following the truck around the Gowrie area. We've decided to trade vehicles every hour just in case this semi driver is brighter than the last one. It appears he is taking the same route as last time.

A couple days later

The driver has followed the same course as the semi driver before him who had the accident, and they have passed the spot where the wind took over last time upending the truck. It looks like the truck is driving across the border now, into Mexico.

I asked Erin if he could identify any of the guys he is working with and all he came up with are Biggs, which we know is Tony Biggins, Low Voice, Jimmy and Cam. Not a lot of help Erin, I think. If this all works the way I want it to though, each of these lowlifes will be arrested at approximately the same time all over the state and into Mexico. We want to be able to see where they are taking these 20 girls and have agents standing by and ready to round up the criminals or follow each of them if they break up the girls with some going one direction and some going another direction. I'm just hoping we are able to arrest every single piece of shit connected to this sex ring and shut it down.

The semi driver drove into a gigantic building and the door was then closed. My agents are surrounding the building with their vehicles with agents all armed to the maximum. We have helicopters in the area as well.

I'm told later that the hour following the semi-truck arriving in Mexico and into the garage was a chaotic cluster. One of the girls in the semi-truck had figured out how to open the zip ties. I had no idea there was a way to do that! She said she used her fingernail and pushed back the stem and was able to move the little box up the stem of the zip tie. With several days to work with, she was able to help the others get out of their constraints as well. Evidently, the 20 girls in the truck had come together with a plan and when the door of the semi was unlocked and opened, the 20 girls, madder than hornets, dove out of the truck together like wild savages. One of the guys got his ear bitten off, one had a torn scrotum, and one had an eyeball dangling on his face. Most of the law breakers had guns but the men were taken so unaware, not many shots were fired. Two of the girls were hit but not seriously wounded.

When my team heard the ruckus, they bulldozed the garage door and after more shooting, were able to round up every single person connected to the ring– 48 in all. And all of them are going down for a very long time. Every single girl of the 20 taken from Iowa were accounted for so none were lost, shot or stolen.

The two girls from the first truck that were rescued a few weeks ago from Fort Dodge, Nancy from Wal-Mart and the pretty brunette from the crusty bar both identified the guys that raped them in the hotel, so those boys were arrested as well. We haven't identified every single name of the 48 arrested, but we do know that the ringleader, Pete, has been identified by our confidential informant who helped us get Erin into this operation. Without him, we would have been at a loss as to when and where this operation was going. I am so relieved that Erin came out of this unscathed and is on his way back to Georgetown.

I would have really liked to have seen the chaos those girls created in the garage in Mexico. There's nothing quite like a pack of mad and angry women who know they have nothing to lose and everything to gain by partnering together to take on the scum of the earth and they did it and did it well! We got them all home to Iowa safe and sound, setting each of them up with counseling if they want it. I think they all realize how very close they came to just being another statistic and lost girl. I'm still amazed at the skill of the girl who figured out how to get those zip ties undone with her fingernail. She said her dad was in law enforcement and had her watch a YouTube video when she was younger, and she remembered it.

CHAPTER 25
Sophie

I am renewed with hope by the generosity of mankind! At least 80% of the businesses I called said they would give a prize, maybe not a $40 prize, but still something, so I ended up with 53 participants on my list for the blood drive prizes. Not too bad, I'm thinking! I am really hoping for at least 300 students to give blood in two weeks.

I was able to make copies of my posters with the website students can sign up for the time that fits their schedule best. They are able to see the prizes that are available to them in the drawing on the website as well. Strike what I said before about this being a job I wouldn't have to spend a lot of time at and still get paid. I haven't been told what I will make yet, but I do know that I have put in a TON of time planning and working this event! And it's not over yet! I do feel happy that this is some of the stuff I love doing—this is my skill set. It's what I do best: planning, organizing, fine tuning, and orchestrating. And I love it.

I get back to the dorm after stapling and taping approximately 100 posters all over campus. I was able to coerce help from a few of the students in my communication class. Of course, there will be payback time at some point where I will have to come through for them as well.

I unlock my dorm door and stutter-step seeing Roy from my speech class (the winker) and Jordan going at it in her bed. I toss my backpack up to my loft and close the door quietly. I check next door to see if Tinsley has eaten supper yet. We enjoy catching each other up on our lives for a bit and I tell her I'm REALLY taking my time because I don't want to walk in again on what I just saw. She laughed and said she has seen it, too, in her room with her roommate.

Tinsley said, "You know, we should be roommates next year! We think alike, our study habits are similar and our morals too!"

I debate whether to tell Tinsley about Bradley's and my plan of possibly getting married this spring or summer since we haven't announced it yet, then decide, what the heck and decide to tell her.

"I'd love that, Tinsley, but I may not be here next year."

"What? Why not? Won't they give you your swimming scholarship back again?" Tinsley asked.

"Oh, I don't know about that, yet, but, my boyfriend, Bradley, asked me to marry him a few weeks ago! I haven't been wearing the ring because we haven't announced it yet. We are trying to figure out if I should transfer to UNI or if he should transfer to ISU and we are thinking of getting married maybe this spring or summer!"

"Congratulations, Sophie!! I am so happy for you," Tinsley shrieked hugging me.

"I'm happy, too, but there is so much to figure out! Bradley thinks it would be more beneficial for me to come his way to UNI since he has a full ride with his tennis scholarship. I'm just not sure, although all my classes but one transfer over to UNI for my communications degree. The one class that doesn't transfer over I can use as an elective, so I don't lose any money and haven't wasted any time. But I like it here, I like my advisor, I like YOU, and my brother is less than a mile away from campus, so it's a lot to think about."

"Well, you guys will figure it out. True love always does," Tinsley said as she fluttered her eyelashes.

"Yes, I am very excited. Bradley and I have been together since 9th grade. We met in our church youth group, and he is the kindest guy I have ever met, besides my brother, Jeremy, that is," I admit.

"You have a brother that is kind? I would like to meet him, please," Tinsley says looking at me seriously.

"Yes, well, he is actually my stepbrother. My dad married Jeremy's birth mom. My stepmom got pregnant in high school and gave up her baby (Jeremy) when she was 18. When Jeremy turned 18, he came to find her to try to get to know her. This all happened about 4 years ago. When I finally met Jeremy, we just clicked."

"Wow, what happened to your real mom or are your parents divorced?" asks Tinsley.

"Hang on to your hat, because here's a story for you," I began. "You may have read about us in the *Fort Dodge Messenger* about four years ago. My mom, Denise, died from a peanut allergy about five years ago and for a long time we really didn't know exactly how she had encountered the peanuts because my dad and I were always very careful about not buying anything with peanuts or nuts of any kind since Mom had such a severe reaction to them. She carried an EpiPen with her ALWAYS."

"Some of the story I was told because I didn't know that my mom was having an affair with her boss, the mayor of our town. She wanted the mayor to divorce his wife and marry her, but the mayor's father-in-law was a senator or something in the government, so he didn't want to burn any bridges because of his political aspirations. I think my mom might have threatened to go public with their affair, so the mayor killed her."

"OH MY GOSH, Sophie!!!!" Tinsley exclaimed. "How did he do it?"

"He bought a can of Planters Peanuts and shook them up with her Folgers brand of coffee, removing the peanuts afterwards. One sip of the tainted, peanut-laden coffee and she was a goner."

"She didn't have time to get to her EpiPen?" Tinsley asked.

"That was probably the final nail in the mayor's coffin—he had taken her EpiPen out of her purse and hid it in his desk drawer at work. My dad and the Chief of Police, Gretchen Knoll set up a sting operation and were able to get the mayor arrested. The Police Chief took a big risk in that if the mayor didn't do it, she would most likely lose her job since the mayor was her boss. My dad and stepmom were so thankful he was caught that they named my little sister, Gretchen, after the Chief of Police, Gretchen Knoll!"

"Wow. That is a story, for sure!" Tinsley said shaking her head. "We just never know what some people have been through, do we?"

"No, we don't. Hey, on another subject, will you give blood in a couple of weeks when the campus blood drive is here?"

Tinsley said, "I don't know. I have never done that before. Will I be able to go to classes afterwards?"

I laughed and said, "Yes, you will eat a cookie or two, drink some juice and water, and be as good as new! Plus, think about all the people you will help with your blood donation. AND it is good for your heart, and it increases blood flow!"

"Well, aren't you a walking advertisement for blood donating! Do you just believe in it so strongly that you are passing this on?" Tinsley asked.

"Yes, I do believe in donating blood, but also I am marketing this event," I replied.

"Really? Wow! I bet that will look good on your resume," Tinsley said.

"My advisor said I will get one credit for coordinating the event. There are other events as well if you want to do one, or we could work together on one—that would be fun! One caution, I didn't think it would take that much time to coordinate, but it DID. It took a LOT of time."

"I'll bet it did," Tinsley smiled. "Were those posters around campus your doing?"

"Yes, you noticed!"

"I did notice all the awesome prizes that people who participate are eligible to win," Tinsley nodded. "Sign me up! I want to win the *Haircut by Marcia* downtown in Ames."

"Here, I'll help you," as I whipped out my phone. "Here's the link, now you have to put in your information about yourself that I don't know."

"Okay. That was pretty easy," Tinsley said after she poked the last button to schedule herself. "My time slot for the blood draw is the first one of the day."

"Just remember to hydrate and eat breakfast, too. That's important. Drink a bottle of water on the way over to Memorial Hall basement where they will be having the blood drive."

"I will. Thanks! I hope I win!" Tinsley grins.

"I hope you do, too, Tins! And if not, you will have done a good thing," I remind her.

"Yes. Do you think your roommate, Jordan, is done by now?" Tinsley asks innocently.

I laugh and say, "I sure hope so, but I did start leaving my swimsuit in my locker room locker, so I'm headed over that way to start practice. See you later and thanks for the good talk and for signing up to donate blood!"

"You are welcome! You are a natural salesperson—who could refuse YOU?!" Tinsley yells after me.

CHAPTER 26
Amber

Maggie is so sad. I want to just take her in my arms and hug her to pieces and make her smile again. My heart is just breaking for her and what Creepy Bob did. But I don't want to make things worse for her and she is trying to find her new normal, so I will go with that.

"Morning, Amber, I see you got your double espresso caramel coffee started already," Maggie said as she glanced at my cup.

"Um hmmm. SOOO good! I couldn't work without it! Although, there for a time, it sure did made me gag," I laugh.

"I know, and you were hardly pregnant but just knew you were pregnant," Maggie said shaking her head.

"Coffee was the trigger, that's for sure!"

"How is Sophie liking ISU? Is she flourishing like we thought she would?" Maggie asked.

"We don't hear from her as much as we'd like to, but we know she is busy, so we try to not bother her. She did call the other day to tell us she is organizing a blood drive on campus and has 150 signed up so far. Her goal on paper is 200 but she said she secretly wants to have 300 show up!"

Maggie asked, "How many attended last year?"

"Sophie said 100 gave blood on campus last year. I think that is a pretty lofty expectation to have 200 more than last year, but what do I know?!" I laughed.

"That sounds like Sophie. The over achiever that she is!" Maggie said with a smile.

"Yes, that can be a good thing and it also can be a bad thing. She drives herself crazy sometimes with the high expectations of herself. Hey, would you and Annie like to come over for supper tomorrow night? We're having ham balls and cheesy potatoes. Josh would really like to not have to eat my ham balls all week long so if you two could come and help us, that would be awesome!"

"Sure, why not?" Maggie said without looking at me. "What time?"

"How about 6PM after you are done here?"

"Perfect. I need to check on the supplies and see how the cleaning gals are doing this morning. I'll be back in about an hour," Maggie said as she scooted away from her desk and me.

I sigh but know I did the right thing in inviting them. Our conversation may be a little touch and go at supper tomorrow, but little Gretchen is AL-WAYS up for entertainment on the spot, so I probably don't need to worry any, I think with a smile. Plus, we are watching our neighbor Nellie's little dog, Gert. Nellie doesn't ask us to doggie sit very often but Gretchen and I just love it when she does. Gert gets along great with Fred, Sophie's fat cat, although Fred just ignores Gert. At least he doesn't pounce on her and hurt her, so I am grateful for that. Gert is just a little fur ball and so very friendly and cuddly.

Fred, Sophie's fat cat, and I had a very tumultuous relationship at the beginning. Every time I would start up the stairs with laundry or whatever, he would attack my ankles leaving me with bleeding wounds. I started carry ammunition with me in my pocket when going up and down the stairs so I could avoid the attacks, tossing little chunks of ham at Fred. It seemed to work, too, but Fred got very large. I think my ham tossing endeared me to him because about six months after I married Josh, Fred finally stopped attacking me, so I didn't have to keep overfeeding him. I have concluded that Fred will live forever, and I've grown to appreciate the furry, aloof feline. He's actually pretty sweet when he wants to be. Occasionally, he even throws himself down in my lap, especially when I am knitting or reading and really don't want him to and takes a nap there. I had wanted to adopt a little dog from *Almost Home*, the animal shelter in town and watched their ads for the longest time but gave up on the idea awhile back after Gretchie was born. I've got my hands full, although I really do love having Gert over for visits!

CHAPTER 27
Sophie

I can't believe it! I keep checking the site and double checking it, but it shows 335 participants that showed up to give blood today! Of course, there will be some that were turned away for one reason or another, but I am so excited! Plus, my advisor even showed up to give blood and afterwards gave me a check for $500 from the school for organizing and promoting the blood drive! She said the communication department has grant money for the events on campus, so she said she was rewarding me for my efforts, saying I went over and beyond what was expected or required. I'm so happy I could cry! I can't wait to tell Jeremy and Bradley!

I head back to my room to study for a test in Modern Literature tomorrow. We had to read a really weird book about existentialism. I personally, don't know how anybody can believe that stuff. It basically just means you live, you exist, you die, and that's it. I need to go over my notes again. I wonder if there are people that really believe this stuff? If I didn't have eternal life figured out with the grace of God and the blood of Jesus, it would be so depressing to me to think that you live, you exist, and you die.

Jordan comes in and with a loud thud drops her books on the floor. Everything about Jordan is loud. I look down from my loft at her and see she is smiling. She starts dancing around and I said, "Geesh, you're happy!"

"YES! I got a C on my algebra test, and I only need a D to pass the class, isn't that great?!"

"Yeah, for sure, Jordan, way to go!" I said as we high-fived.

"And, I've got a boyfriend," Jordan sings as she dances now.

"Ahh. Roy from my speech class, right?" I ask.

"Yeah, but I didn't know you knew Roy," Jordan said.

"Yup. I don't know him well, but I met him the first day of class since we both got to speech class before it started. I don't think I've talked to him since then, though."

"Hey, Jordan, can you help me with something? I am in charge of the prizes for donating blood on campus this year. Can you give me 53 numbers between 1 and 335 and I'll circle them on my numbered spread sheet; they will be the winners of the prizes."

"Sure! Hey, I forgot to go over and give blood, can I still get a prize?" Jordan asked.

"No. What is the first number?" I asked.

"Damn. I always forget about that stuff," Jordan sulked.

After I got the 53 numbers from Jordan, I started matching them up with girl and boy prizes. I came to Tinsley since her number was called, so I hook her up with a *Haircut by Marcia* that she wanted to win, as I smile to myself.

"Hey, Jordan, what is Roy's last name?"

"Roy...I don't know. I have his cell#, though. I'll text him. Why do you want to know—you writing a book or something?" Jordan asks me.

"Roy Klindt just won the oil change at Arnold's Motor Supply. He gave blood today. There are a couple of guys named Roy that gave blood, so I just thought if your guy was Roy Klindt, you could tell him."

"It IS Klindt! I'm texting him that he won!" Jordan shouts with a fist in the air.

"Yea!" I say as I continue to match up donors with prizes.

My number is one of the numbers Jordan gave me, but I decide to give my prize to my advisor since she set me up with this gig. She will win....the new fragrance from *Bath, Body, and Beyond.*

***

After my Modern Lit test and class the following day, Roy catches up with me as I'm walking out and asks me where Arnold's Motor Supply is. I tell him I just sent out an email this morning before class to all the blood donors thanking them for giving blood and I named the winners, their prize, and the address to pick up their prize.

"Hey, do you want to go with me to get my prize? I don't know Ames that well so can you direct me?" Roy asked.

I remember my gut and the reaction I felt when Roy winked at me the first day of class and how I hated it and feel like winkers are not good characters. Then I think, well, I kind of know him—he's in my speech class, he is kinda dating Jordan and he gave blood. Most people that give blood are good people, right? So, I say, "Ok, but only if you can take me to *Bath, Body, and Beyond* after we get your oil changed. I don't have a vehicle and I want to pick up my advisor's prize to give to her. I've got classes until lunch. How about we meet after lunch to go?"

"Let's meet in parking lot H—you can ride the Cy Bus over there. I've got a white Prius and I'll be watching for you. I'll even buy you a burger so we can go as soon as you are done with your morning classes and skip campus lunch."

"And French fries?" I ask innocently.

"Yup. See you about 12:00," Roy said as he turned to get to his next class.

I get to my next class a little late even though I ran most of the way. It seems kind of weird to me that Roy wanted to ride the Cy bus separately but maybe he doesn't want it to look like a date or something. I'll have to tell him I have a boyfriend and put his mind at ease, I think to myself, as I open my textbook.

CHAPTER 28
Roy

I skipped the rest of my classes this morning. I had to get stuff ready. I had been thinking about this for a while ever since I had to let go of Cynthia Coate, the lifeguard from Furman Aquatic Center, the Ames swimming pool, early in September. I was able to keep Cynthia for over a month, but I saw some kids sniffing around the place and had to get rid of her shortly after school started. I miss my daily fuck or two with her. I can't go back to the old, abandoned building I found on the farmhouse lot that nobody was living in anymore. It has no heat and I plan to keep Sophie a long while, so I will most likely need some heat and some running water, too. The place that I scoped out a few weeks ago just might be the ticket—Furman Aquatic Center. It closed the last part of August. I'm hoping it still has electricity, but I need to check that out and get some supplies hauled in there so I can safely leave Sophie in there without someone hearing or seeing her. That first day I met her I knew I had to have her—she looked so similar to Cynthia it was eerie. She didn't warm up to me, though, but this is working out perfectly--more perfect than I ever thought possible.

Meeting Jordan and getting into Sophie's room was crucial! I was able to find out that Sophie was having the blood drive, so I signed up for it and who would guess that I would win something and be able to convince her to ride with me in my car to get my prize? My luck is so strong right now. I should go play the horses or something!

I wish I didn't have to do this in quite so much of a hurry, because haste makes waste, but the timing was just too perfect to give up and I may never get this good of an opportunity again. I am thinking if Sophie doesn't get back to the dorm for lunch, she most likely won't tell anyone she is meeting me and going with me. If we arrive separately to the parking lot on the Cy Bus, nobody will remember seeing us together. And if nobody sees us together, nobody will suspect me as her kidnapper or eventually her murderer. That makes me sad, thinking about murdering Sophie. I hope I don't have to do that for a very long time. As long as she cooperates, I can keep her alive. OK, stop daydreaming, I tell myself! Think about what you need to go buy instead. I need rope, a pail, zip ties, what else, what else. Maybe a blanket, and bottled water in case the city has turned off the water. Off I go to Menards.

About 11:30 I ride the Cy Bus over to Parking Lot H to find my car and get in position. I have my chloroform ready, and Sophie won't know what hit her until it's too late. About 12:05 I see Sophie step off the Cy Bus and look around for me. I step out of my car and wave to her to flag her over. When she gets in the car and buckles up, I ask her to reach something in my back seat for me that I forgot. As she turns her head toward me, I am able to get her chloroformed and that will keep her unconscious until after I unload her at the Aquatic Center where I have set up shop.

I made a little jail in the checkroom area where people generally pay their money to get into the pool to swim so Sophie can't get out and run away from me when I'm not there. I plan to still go to classes, so nobody suspects me of the kidnapping. This way I can visit Sophie between classes, after classes and on weekends, too. This is so exciting!

This is exactly how I felt when I first captured Cynthia Coate. I had been watching her every day I went to the Ames pool last summer. Girls like her don't go out with guys like me so I didn't even trouble myself to ask her—I already knew what her answer would be. Instead, I TOOK her, and I loved every single minute of it. Not sure she would agree to that, I thought chuckling. Man, the police and special forces were all over the area I dumped her. They were not even CLOSE to finding out where it happened and where I held her hostage until I had to kill her and leave her to be found in the ditch. Too bad they aren't as smart as me, the morons.

I wish I could have used the same location as last time, the abandoned farm building where nobody lives. I liked being separate from everyone way out in the country. It was safer and I had less of a chance of getting caught. I'll just have to gag Sophie when I am not with her so she can't make too much noise, but it should still work. I checked and they still have electricity there so I should be able to start a space heater for her when I leave her in the evenings, so she doesn't freeze. I am so compassionate. Sophie should appreciate me and my goodness very much.

I've got her in my fashioned jail. I am debating whether to leave her books in there, so she has something to do. Again, I pat myself on the back telling me what a good, compassionate guy I am! I decide not to give her the books, however, but I may give them to her later as a bargaining chip. It's good to make your victims appreciate everything you do for them. I will wait and feed her in a few days when she is good and hungry, so she appreciates me even more.

I dig through Sophie's purse and find her phone. Jordan told me that Sophie has a boyfriend and is talking to him ALL the time. I flip through their conversations and see that they are planning to

get married. Gee, I hope my plan does not inter-
fere with theirs, I think with a laugh. Oh my. I
see that Sophie and Bradley ALMOST had sex. Well,
I'm going to make SURE that happens, Bradley,
my boy—with ME! I decide to send Bradley a text

from Sophie's phone. I text, "B-so sorry, having 2nd
thoughts of marrying u. Pls don't call me—I won't
answer. Need time to sort stuff out. Soph." I hit
send. I think that should buy me a little time before
people start thinking she is missing.

Sophie starts to stir. I quickly put her gag in her
mouth. Her zip tied hands are behind her. She tries
to sit up and looks at me with huge eyes and confusion.

"Well, hello there, beautiful! Welcome to my dun-
geon! You and I are going to be best friends by the
time this is all over! I know I promised you a burger
and fries, and maybe if you are a good girl, I will
feed you tomorrow. I do have some water here for
you. If I take the gag off, will you promise not to
scream?"

Sophie nods her head and I remove her gag. She
says, "Roy, why are you doing this? Why?"

"Oh, dear Sophie, I have been biding my time waiting for the perfect opportunity to have you for my
very own. It did take a few months, but I am just
positive you will be worth the wait. I do hope you
haven't made any plans for the next few months

because I'm afraid you will have to cancel them, my love."

"What?! Roy? What are you talking about? You can't keep me here! This is illegal. People will be looking for me. You won't get away with this!" Sophie starts screaming so loud she almost bursts my ear drums.

I punch Sophie in the mouth to stop her screaming and put her gag back on, which catches the blood spatter. "Too bad you didn't cooperate, Sophie. Now you will not get your water break. Ahhh. Maybe tomorrow, yes? IF you are a good girl, that is. There is a pail in the corner for you to use for your bathroom and look, Sophie, I am a kind person. I even brought you a blanket. Let's work on your kindness, can we, Sophie? You need to appreciate what I give you, because I don't have to give you SQUAT! You understand, you dirty little skank? I AM IN CONTROL, and YOU need to remember that. I'll check on you tomorrow to see if you are in a better frame of mind. Goodbye, Sophie darling."

As I close and lock the door with the new padlock I got at Menards, I hear Sophie's muffled cries. I did good. This place will work just great! I can make it to my 2:00 speech class if I hurry, I think.

CHAPTER 29
Bradley

What the ... why would Sophie send me this text? We were in a good place this morning when I talked to her. What could have happened between then and now? Why would she need some time to think? And what is she trying to sort out? I dial her number and I get her voice mail. I'm pacing the floor of my room. I don't understand. Maybe Jeremy has some answers for me. I'm going to call him.

"Hey, Jeremy? It's Bradley. You heard from Sophie today?"

"No. I talked to her yesterday, though. Why? What's up?" Jeremy asks.

"Well, I just got a text that said she can't marry me, and she needs some time to sort stuff out and not to call her. I called her anyway and just got her voice mail. I just wondered if she had said anything to you about what's going on and to see if you know what she is trying to sort out?"

"Oh man, I'm so sorry," said Jeremy. "I don't know

anything, and this surprises me as much as it surprises you. It really doesn't sound like something Sophie would do; do you think?"

"No, she would never break up with me through a text. That just isn't Sophie. Plus, I hope she will never break up with me, PERIOD, but to do it over text just seems very out of character of her," I said.

"Will you let me know if you find out anything, Jeremy?"

"Absolutely, Bradley. So sorry you are going through this, man."

CHAPTER 30
Sophie

I can't believe this is happening to me. My dad warned me over and over about trusting my gut and I didn't listen. I had a bad feeling the minute Roy the creep winked at me and I went with him anyway. I don't think anybody saw us either, I think, as my eyes fill again with tears. Roy is going to get away with this and there is nothing I can do!

I sniff and look around at my surroundings, trying to find something, ANYTHING that can help me with an escape. I hoist myself to my feet, but it looks like the windows are all boarded up. I don't even know where I am, but it looks similar to the Aquatic Center in Fort Dodge where I worked last summer with all the baskets in the slots for kids to store their valuables while swimming. Outside my jail cell there is a case of water—wish I could reach it now. I also see a space heater—wish I had that as well. I slide down the wall again to the cement floor, crestfallen. I'm cold, hungry, and I see no way out of this. Think, Sophie, think, I tell myself. There has to be a way. I pull on my zip ties and that only seems to make them tighter practically cutting off my blood flow.

I must have dozed off as it's starting to get dark now. I start to cry even though nobody can hear me or see me or ever will, I think sadly. I start thinking about my first mom, Denise, and how I lost her to her peanut allergy. I hated that she cheated on my dad, but she and my dad were not very compatible; they argued all the time. I do have some good memories, though. I try to focus on them and good things, like when she used to push me on the swings when I was little or when she took me shopping. I haven't thought about her for a very long time. Will I soon be dead like her?

I wake up again and it is still dark, and I have to pee —really bad. I know Roy said there was a pail in the corner, but I can't see it; it's too dark. I'll have to see if I can feel along the wall for it. There it is--I found it! With my hands secured in back, I can't unzip my jeans. But there is enough stretch in my jeans, I am able to pull them down to my ankles from the back before I sit on the pail. But, now to get them up again, how am I going to do that? I turn the jeans around with my foot so I can reach the zipper and unzip and unbutton them. Now I can pull them up again, but I can't work the zipper now that it's in the front again. I'll just have to leave them open.

I hear a car pull up outside. I start trying to yell

but my cries are so muffled I'm sure they can't be heard outside. I hear the padlock open outside and in walks Roy.

"I trust you slept well, my beautiful Sophie?" I gave you your first night off but now that you had the evening to yourself, you must share yourself with me," Roy says grinning at me.

I feel like puking and then get scared that if I puke, I might choke on it because of the gag in my mouth. Instead, I look at Roy with more hate than I have ever had in my entire life. If my eyes could kill him, he would be DEAD.

"Not talking, little one? I think I can make your life a little easier if you can learn to cooperate and be appreciative. How about if I take your gag off? Would you like that? Maybe you'd like a drink of water today?"

I nod even though I literally hate this guy's guts. Roy takes off my gag and brings the bottle of water to my lips. I gulp and gulp greedily almost choking. Roy puts the lid back on the water and said, "I can leave the rest of the water with you, Sophie if you can show me some cooperation. I'm going to cut your zip ties on your feet, ok?" Roy takes out his pocketknife and slits the ties, sticking the knife back into his pocket. "Does that feel better without your feet tied together, Sophie? Now, I'm going to slide your jeans and underwear down so I can have a better look at you, ok?"

I start to scream, and Roy immediately shoves the gag back into my mouth and continues to shove my pants down and off my legs. I try kicking and screaming and fighting...and crying...as he humps over me with guttural sounds. I turn my head to the side and puke. And this time I don't care if I choke on my puke and die. I don't even care. I don't hear what Roy says or does after that. He leaves me in his jail in a heap with puke in my mouth and on my gag, locks the door and leaves.

I don't know how long I lay there on the cold, concrete floor. I'm losing track of time and losing track of myself. Nobody is ever going to find me. Nobody. Not Jeremy, Bradley, Mom, Dad, Gretchen. They will all go on with their lives and I will not be a part of any of it anymore, I think as I sob uncontrollably. How long will this go on I wonder.

I pray like I have never prayed before. I feel Jeremy praying with me and I close my eyes and concentrate. I feel Him talking to me and comforting me with a God hug, telling me to be strong and that He is with me. I cry myself to sleep.

CHAPTER 31
Jeremy

I'm getting worried, too. Sophie generally texts me or calls me at least once a day and I haven't heard from her for over 24 hours now. Something is wrong--really wrong. I tried texting Sophie and she responded, "Don't bother me, Jeremy. I'm busy figuring stuff out." That just doesn't sound like Sophie and what she would say. So, I tried calling her and it went straight to voice mail. I decide to talk to her swim coach and find out she wasn't at practice last night or this morning. That is so unlike Sophie to skip practice, especially a couple in a row. Something is not right. I'm calling Josh.

"Josh. It's me, Jeremy."

"Hello, Jeremy? How's it going?" Josh answered.

"Not good, Josh. Something is wrong here," I said.

"What's wrong, Jeremy? What's going on?" Josh asked a little more guarded now.

I sigh and tell Josh about Bradley's call to me and

the text he and I both sent to Sophie and what it said. I felt I had to tell Josh about Bradley's proposal because it may have something to do with why Sophie is not responding. I hope WHEN we find Sophie (Not IF we find Sophie), she will understand why I had to divulge their secret.

"Jeremy, sit tight. Help is on the way," Josh said and hung up.

I called Bradley and told him I had still not heard from Sophie and that I called her coach and told Bradley what he said. Then I told him Josh is coming and that I felt I had to tell him their secret since we can't find Sophie.

"Why'd you do that, man? You know we were going to announce it at Christmas! Why'd you have to ruin it all?" Bradley yells into the phone.

"I'm so sorry, Bradley, but it may be the reason Sophie disappeared. We need to be as honest as we can with the police when they get here and I thought that might be important, so I told him what our texts said, including yours. Your text didn't make sense if I didn't tell him what it was about--marrying you."

Bradley is silent at the other end of the line and finally says, "I get it, Jeremy. Sorry I went off on you like that. The important thing right now is that we find Sophie, whether she wants to marry me or not. I think maybe I should come to Ames."

"Let me check with Josh when he gets here, Bradley. I'm sure he will want to talk to you at some point, but he may just call you. I'll let you know as soon as I hear anything more, okay? For now, just stay put."

CHAPTER 32
Josh

I knew I should not have let my sweet little girl go to college. It's just too big and there are too many shits in the world for it to be a safe place for her. The last murder we had in Ames was the Cynthia Coate murder around the beginning of the school year, and she looked so much like Sophie. I should have insisted she come home right that minute I realized the uncanny resemblance. But I didn't and now look what's happened? My Sophie....my sweet Sophie!

I need to get hold of myself or I'll be no help to anyone. Fortunately, I was able to get my boss to let me lead this investigation since I AM the lead investigator of DCI, but he said if I start acting irrationally, he will immediately pull me off the case. He called the Ames police department and told them what is going on. They started in on how we needed to wait 48 hours and my boss shut him down fortunately.

I have to keep my head about me and think. I've got

my team pulled together and we are almost at the university now. I had Sophie's phone reviewed to see where the last ping came from. It was from the ISU campus when Jeremy heard from her—IF that was Sophie that was doing the texting. I also have some of my men scouting the area around the campus, looking into all the vacant homes and buildings. I'm on my way to talk to the roommate.

I knock on Sophie's dorm room and finally a big girl opens the door in what seems like forever. She's rubbing her eyes like she just got up even though it's about noon. I look past her and see what a pigsty the room is in and remember Sophie telling us about her roommate, Jordan, and her messy habits. "Jordan? I'm Sophie's dad, Josh Jackson."

"Ok.....," Jordan mumbles with a confused look on her face.

"I have a few questions about the whereabouts of Sophie. Can I come in and talk to you for a few minutes?" I asked.

"Yeah, but I haven't seen Sophie since the night before last," Jordan said.

"Was she happy, sad, what was she doing when you last saw her?" I asked.

"She had me help her choose the winners of the blood drive. She was pretty stoked. I gave her 53 numbers and she matched them up with the numbers on her spreadsheet to give them a prize. She was working on emails to all the 300 or so participants letting them know who the winners were and what they were winning."

"How about after that?" I asked.

"I left the room about 11PM and she was still typing her emails. When I came back about 3AM, she was asleep. I assumed she went to her 8AM class the next morning since she wasn't here when I woke up yesterday morning."

"And that was the last time you saw her then, 11PM on Tuesday night? She didn't text you or call you? You don't know anything that was bothering her?"

"Nope. We're not besties, just roommates," Jordan replies.

I nod and say, "Thanks, Jordan, I may need to talk to you again, but thank you for your help today."

"You're welcome. I hope you find her."

Next, I drive over to Jeremy's and let him know what we have found out so far. "Do you really think Sophie was upset by the marriage proposal, Jeremy? I just don't think that makes sense to me why Sophie would disappear from everything."

Jeremy replied, "No, I don't think that is it, either. Sophie would not have skipped swim practice twice in a row, skipped all her classes and quit talking to all of us. That's just not her. When Sophie had a problem in the past, she liked to talk to me. Sometimes I didn't even help her solve it, but she said just talking out loud to a good listener—is what she called me, always helped her. This is just not like her at all."

"I know you two were close, Jeremy. That's why I wanted to come and talk to you. I think you know Sophie even better than Bradley."

"I do know that Sophie did go to Wednesday morning's swim practice since I called her coach to find out the last time he saw her. So sometime after swim practice, then breakfast, and then Modern Lit class Wednesday is when she seems to possibly have disappeared," I told Josh. "But I haven't heard back from her other three classes following speech to see if she attended them as well. I left messages, though."

"Good leg work, Jeremy. I appreciate it. I'm going to talk to her Modern Lit teacher and see if she/he can shed any light on this. I'll talk to you later."

CHAPTER 33
Roy

I can hardly sit through class knowing what I have back at the Aquatic Center waiting for me. This is the life I say to myself! I AM IN CONTROL! I absolutely love it! I think I'll skip lunch and have a little nooner, I think rubbing my hands together in glee.

After I sent a text message to Sophie's boyfriend, Bradley and Jeremy, whoever that guy is, I smashed her phone to bits so nobody will be able to contact her or locate her by any pings. I watch a lot of movies. I know how this all works, ha!

"Oh, Sophie!! I'm BAAAAACK!" I say as I unlock the Aquatic Center door and let myself in. "Did you have a good morning? I had to come back for more because I missed you so much!"

"Ooooh, ick. You smell like puke. It must be on your gag. Now, if I take your gag out, do you promise not to scream and throw a fit?"

Sophie nods. I open her bottle of water and give her a drink, which she drinks thirstily. I remember not leaving her any in her jail cell because she screamed, but she wouldn't have been able to drink it anyway with her hands behind her back. She's not to be trusted yet, I can tell. I need to break her down further before I can trust her.

"You were thirsty, weren't you? I brought you the hamburger and fries I promised you the other day. And hey! I got my oil changed, too, from Arnolds Motor Supply. That saved me some bucks, let me tell you! So, thank you for pulling my name out of your hat and choosing me. I'm just giving you a bite or two for now, ok?" I said as I wrap up the rest of the burger and fries after feeding Sophie a couple of bites of each. "Now, you know what's next, right?" I asked.

"Please, no, Roy. Please. Don't do this to me," Sophie pleaded.

"Awww. Come on, it's nothing you haven't done before. You can share with me. I won't even tell," I whispered.

Sophie shakes her head, starts to cry and hiccup. I can't stand it and put a clean gag in her mouth, so I don't have to smell her puke or listen to her whining. Then I mount her and ride her like there's no tomorrow. She's such a bad little bitch.

CHAPTER 34
Sophie

I don't know how many days have passed; I'm losing track. I feel hungry and sick to my stomach at the same time. And I'm cold all the time. I find the blanket Roy left me and try to wind it around me the best I can. I try to think of the past and the fun experiences to keep my mind occupied and to keep me from going crazy, although I might be there anyway, I think sadly.

I pray and talk to God a lot. I know He's helping me through this. He gave me a safe place to go with my mind the last time Roy was here. I hardly knew Roy was even on top of me. I try to go to that safe space now, but He won't let me. Instead, I focus on Bradley—no, that's too hard. We made a pact long ago that we would save ourselves for each other. Well, that pact went down the toilet. I can't even think about Bradley right now. He will never understand all of this. I start to cry and can't seem to get hold of myself. I almost throw up again but am able to force it down to my stomach again.

I notice that Roy has plugged in the space heater and it's running. It's definitely warmer and better than yesterday. I try again to think of important people and events and cheer myself up and think of Jeremy and his kindness. I sometimes wish Jeremy wasn't my brother. He is exactly the whole package and whoever ends up with Jeremy is a lucky girl. I hope I am there to see it, I think sadly, and tears start to form again. I shake my head, rolling my eyes to the ceiling to help stop my tears and think of little Gretchen and her beautiful, brown eyes, her expressions, her love. Again, I start with the tears. Maybe I need to think of stuff that WON'T make me sad and instead make me MAD, like ROY.

I've noticed that Roy left his knife that he cuts my feet apart each day safely out of my reach outside my jailed in area, but if I can just get my hands apart, maybe I can reach it and spring the lock. I'm dreaming I know, because if I can't get my hands undone, I can't do any of this. There's GOT to be a way to get these stupid zip ties off. I look down at my ankles and lying on my back I can almost reach them, but not quite. I sigh, feeling helpless and hopeless. "God, please help me!" I cry.

Roy is back. He unwraps my cold hamburger and fries from earlier and tries to feed me again. I eat, knowing I need to be strong if I'm ever to get out of this place. I just have to wait for the right time. Roy gives me water next, and I gulp again, thirstily.

He then checks my poop/pee pail and said I need to drink more water.

"If I zip tie your hands in the front today, can I trust you to be a good girl?" Roy asked.

I nod.

"Ok, then, I'll leave you a bottle of water and the rest of your lunch from earlier. We don't want you to get too weak and dehydrated now, do we?" Roy asked with a crazy grin.

"Spread 'em girl. You know what I want now. You should know the routine by now," Roy coaxes.

I turn my head, close my eyes, and go to my safe place again and it's peaceful, serene and beautiful. I see my first mom there smiling at me and telling me it's going to be okay. There are rivers and sailboats in my safe place and lots of furry animals that all come to me, unafraid. I sit down and stroke them all and hold them to me, hugging them. I sing the songs I learned and know from church. "My God is an awesome God, he reigns from heaven above. With wisdom, power, and love, our God is an awesome God."

When I get back from my safe place, Roy is gone, and my hands are zip tied in front of me instead of in back of me. I can move my shoulders now; they were so sore in that position for so long. I see the bottle of water Roy left and greedily open it and drink it all. I stop and bow my head and thank God for my hands in front of me now and for the water that quenched my thirst. Now, I need to get to work on a plan on how to get out of here.

CHAPTER 35
Maggie

My turn to hug and soothe Amber. She's a hot mess and I would be too, if it was my Annie that was missing. Amber insisted on coming into work today even though I told her to take some more time off. She said she can't just sit at home and think about Sophie, and that she needed a better distraction. She said little Gretchen keeps asking, "Mommy sad?" and "Mommy cryin'?" and pats her on the back. That makes ME tear up.

Josh is keeping Amber up to date on everything so that is good, but it just seems like Sophie disappeared into thin air. No trace of her. Josh is still in the process of going to each of Sophie's morning classes and interviewing the students in those classes.

CHAPTER 36
Josh

A girl that sat by Sophie during world history class on Wednesday said she had asked Sophie to go to lunch that day and Sophie said she had to go with a guy to get his oil changed. I talked to Jeremy who told me it wasn't he who needed his oil changed. I'm going back to the roommate, Jordan, to see if she can be of any help.

I'm on my way back to Sophie's dorm to see if her roommate or any of the other girls in her wing of the dorm know who Sophie might have gone with to get his oil changed. Jordan doesn't answer the door, so I move further up the hallway and start knocking on doors. I've checked with everyone who answered their door, and nobody knows who Sophie may have gone with. I go back to Sophie's room and Jordan is back now. I'm not very hopeful since Jordan wasn't very helpful the first time, but I ask her anyway.

"No, I don't ...wait. You said an oil change? The

night before she disappeared, I was helping Sophie draw names for prizes of the people that gave blood. My boyfriend, Roy, won a prize to get his oil changed. Do you want me to call him to see if he knows anything?"

"Yes, please, Jordan, that would be very helpful," I said.

"It's going into voice mail, but I'll leave him a message. Roy? Jordan here. Hey, remember my roommate, Sophie? She's been missing since Wednesday and her dad is here looking for her. He said someone in her world history class said she was going with a guy to get his oil changed after classes. Would that have been you since you won the free oil change at Arnolds Motor Supply because you gave blood? Call me back. Sophie's dad would like to talk with you to see if you know anything that can help. Thanks."

"Thank you, Jordan. Do you know Roy's last name and schedule and where he would be right now?"

"His last name is Klindt, but sorry, I don't know his schedule. We just started dating and I haven't seen him since last weekend," Jordan said.

"No problem. And thanks again. I'll take it from here."

My next stop is the registrar to find out this boy, Roy's schedule.

CHAPTER 37
Sophie

I know I'll only have one shot at this, so if I can figure out how to get out of these zip ties, I'll have to make this work; otherwise, I'm pretty sure I will be a dead girl as soon as Roy gets tired of me.

Since Roy left me today with my hands bound in front of me instead of back, I have a chance to look more closely at the zip ties around my hands and feet. Somehow, I feel that little box on the zip tie has GOT to be the key to loosening the zip tie. I play around with it for what seems like hours and make the zip tie tighter, not the direction I want to go. I stick my fingernail down in that little box and I bend the strap of the zip tie down. I can actually move the zip tie UP!! I scramble out of the hand zip tie and work on my feet and am able to remove that one much faster than the first one. I'm able to pick the lock on the makeshift jail Roy had me in with the end of the zip tie. I run to the door, even though I know Roy has a padlock on it from the outside. It doesn't budge even an inch. I'll have to wait for Roy, and I'll have to be ready for my one time shot at getting out of this alive.

I know I will never be able to outrun Roy. He's been feeding me practically nothing, so I know I don't have the strength. That leaves the element of surprise and maybe a move or two my one-armed self-defense teacher taught me. First, I need to look around and find something heavy to knock Roy out with or at least deter him. I find a broom—that's not a lot of help. Ah ha! I found an old-fashioned cash register on a shelf, but can I even lift it? I can! But I need more. If I'm not able to swing it and hit him with it with full force, it's not going to knock him out, so what else can I use in this building?

My backpack! It's in the corner and I have my can of mace in there that my dad insisted I take to college! That will be perfect! What else? I see Roy's pocket-knife that was out of my reach before when I was zip tied inside his makeshift jail. I put that in my pocket as well. I see some floating buoys and rope on the very top shelf that have seen better years. Maybe I can take off the buoys and use that rope, too. I wish I had watched more old MacGyver episodes! He was so good at making something out of nothing!

I start removing all the buoys from the rope and find various little spaces to stash the buoys in so that Roy won't see them when he first opens the door. Luckily, Jeremy once showed me how to make a noose for a school play I was in during high school. I tied a noose and am trying to play out in my head how this could go.

If Roy steps through the door and I can get the noose to fall down around his head...Ok. I need a ladder to be taller than Roy. I find a small step ladder shoved under some towels and decide it will have to do. I put it behind the door and get my heavy cash register to the top step of the small step ladder. I take the noose and the rest of the rope and string it around the broom handle so it will stay tight and string it further to a rafter, knowing I won't be able to hang on to it most likely if Roy gets the upper hand. The broom will help me keep the rope tight. The noose and rope may not hang Roy but should at least keep him in place so that he can't go after me if this works and I can get away.

I take the towels and try to form the shape of a body out of it to put under the blanket Roy left me, so it looks like I am on the floor sleeping right where he left me. Is it good enough, though? My plan has all kinds of gaping holes in it. Please, God, this just HAS to work!

CHAPTER 38
Roy

I look at my phone and listen to Jordan's voice mail. That stupid BITCH! She just wrecked my whole plan. I could KILL THE FAT SKANK! Talking to myself, I say, "Calm down, Roy, calm down." I guess the best thing to do is call Jordan and see if she has Sophie's dad's phone number and get it over with. I am a good actor, always have been. It's been my best attribute for years! But the sad thing is, my time is already up with Sophie. I'll have to kill her tonight. I can't have her telling anyone what happened, so I hate it, but I have to do it tonight. I only got to enjoy beautiful Sophie for three days. But I gotta do what I gotta do.

I don't think Sophie's dad suspects a thing, unless HE is also a good actor! I chuckle. I told him I did get my oil changed at Arnolds Motor Supply on Tuesday and he can talk to Jay at Arnolds and he will confirm that I was alone. I tell Sophie's dad that I saw Sophie in speech class Tuesday morning, but not since then. I'm such a good liar! I was even able to squeeze out a few tears to really win an OSCAR!

Now I need to figure out how I'm going to kill Sophie and where I will put her afterwards. I guess I can just kill her in the Aquatic Center and leave her there. That could work. But maybe there would be some DNA or something in the building I left behind that they would find linking the murder to me. I think I need to do it after dark tonight. I'll strangle her like I did Cynthia after one final fuck and find a deep ditch to toss her in. That should work. I'm sad thinking about it. But there are lots more pretty girls where those came from, I think to myself.

CHAPTER 39
Josh

"Jeremy, do you want to go on a stakeout with me tonight?"

"Sure, do you have a lead on Sophie's kidnapping?" Jeremy asked.

"Well, it's just a hunch right now, but if my hunch is right, the guy that got his oil changed is going to take us to Sophie tonight."

"Really? Tell me what happened!" Jeremy said.

"I talked to Roy Klindt, Sophie's roommate's boyfriend. He was the one who won the free oil change at Arnolds Motor Supply. It's GOT to be him. I've been doing some checking on him after I interviewed him. He has a juvenile record about a mile long and a history of animal abuse as well. He assaulted several girls in high school, and he did some time in juvie for it. He lives at home with his mom, and he is 25 years old now. I couldn't find the mother at the house but poked around there a little. Sophie isn't there. He's got her somewhere else my gut is telling me."

"He sounds like a lovely specimen to mankind. Let's nail him. What time we going?"

"I found out what car Roy is driving and where he parks it. I'll be in Lot H, watching his car this afternoon. I do have a tracker on his car as well, so if he gets in his car, I'll be following him, but I think he'll wait until it's dark. If you want to meet me here about 9:00 tonight, that would be perfect."

"I'll be there," Jeremy confirmed.

CHAPTER 40

Jeremy

I hope this plan of Josh's works. I can't even think about Sophie not being okay. I've been praying every single day, practically every single minute since I suspected she was missing. I'm so glad I called Josh and he came so quickly. Sophie just HAS to be alive yet. I know God has a plan for her. I don't know what the plan is, but I just know that I love that girl with all my heart; she's precious. And I know that God loves her even more than I do, so that is comforting. He will watch over her and keep her safe until we can get her rescued. I have to believe that.

As I am putting together some sandwiches and making a thermos full of coffee for tonight's stakeout, I am very thankful that Josh is letting me participate. I just hope and pray this ends well.

CHAPTER 41
Roy

I'd better get going to see Sophie. I'm not happy about the situation. I really thought I would have her a hell of a lot longer than three measly days, but it is what it is, and I don't want to get caught. I've got my cord in my pocket to choke her and will carry her out to my car to put her in my trunk. Then Sophie and I will take a lovely trip to the country where I will find a comfortable ditch for my beloved Sophie to decay in. It was nice while it lasted!

As I walk to the aquatic door, I think of my mom and what a pain in the butt she was all my life. Always nagging at me, "Roy, can't you do anything right?" or "Roy, I'm so ashamed of you." Well, I don't have to listen to her bitchin' anymore. I took care of that several months ago. I thought she would appreciate my gesture of knowing the place she would like best to finally lie at rest. I quietly dug a hole in our backyard for nights on end, right under her nose—she didn't even notice it! She was so busy watching her stupid soapies and drinking herself into oblivion that if she saw her grave, she apparently didn't know what or who it was for. What a bitch. Glad she is out of the way, and I have my own space now.

As I open the door, I see that Sophie is right where I left her this morning. Oh, shoot! I should have brought a "last meal" for her to enjoy before the kill, but I forgot. Oh well, she won't be alive that much longer and that probably would have cost me $10. $10 is $10. Money don't grow on trees as my mom told me day in and day out whenever I asked her for some. As I move to close the aquatic door, a thick rope drops over my neck. I look up to see where it came from and am sprayed in the eyes with something. I feel blinded; I can't see! Out of the corner of my blurred vision, I see something large and metal coming my way. I'm so dizzy I can't get out of the way in time and then...darkness.

CHAPTER 42
Josh

"Jeremy, we're going to go get Sophie—I am that sure of it!" I said as Jeremy got into my vehicle. "Roy left about two minutes ago, and the tracker shows him heading to 13th Street. My technician just called me and told me that he was able to pick up a ping from his phone in that area several times in the last few days."

I squeal out of the parking lot in route to 13th Street. I've already called for backup and the Ames police force should be arriving shortly.

"The Furman Aquatic Center?? THAT's where he's been keeping her?! I can't believe we missed this! Jeremy, you stay put. The door is open and I'm going in. My guys will be here shortly. Just stay safe."

"Okay," Jeremy replied.

I take my gun out of its holster and take off the safety, creeping into the building where I find Roy hanging from a rafter, but on his tip toes with a noose around his neck and a lump the size of Rhode Island on his forehead. I look around and don't see Sophie anywhere. I keep my gun trained on the direction of Roy but step out of the building. I see Jeremy opening his arms wide as Sophie runs into them. I'm so relieved that my knees buckle. Down on my knees, I say, "Thank you, thank you, Lord. I am your faithful servant from this day going forward, I promise. Thank you for keeping my Sophie alive. Amen."

I motion the officers into the building where Roy is still dangling from the rafter on his tip toes so as not to choke to death. He's complaining of a massive headache. I'd like to give Roy something else to complain about!

I tell Sophie I love her and the three of us are in a group hug crying our eyes out. Jeremy and Sophie ride with me to the police station where we need to process Sophie and question her. She will then have to go to the hospital to be examined. I know she just wants to go home and crawl into her bed and pull a blanket over her head, but we have to get this over with.

Sophie told us about the blood drive and the prizes. She mentioned going with Roy because she didn't have a car and she wanted to pick up her prize and give it to her advisor who assigned her the blood drive project. I'm so ashamed. Sophie didn't have

a car because I SPENT THE CAR FUND ON GAM-
BLING. I vow to never, EVER, EVER gamble again. It
ALMOST cost me the most precious thing I have—
my daughter.

When Sophie arrived at the hospital, she was given
an exam and offered emergency care for protec-
tion against sexual assault. After hearing the spiel,
Sophie agreed to take the emergency contraceptive
pills which are high doses of oral contraceptives or
the pill that millions of women take every day. I
was not aware that this type of pill is not to be
confused with RU-486 or the early abortion pill. I
thought they were one and the same. At least pregnancy by this lunatic is one thing Sophie will not
have to worry about going forward. I know she is
going to need lots of therapy after going through
this horrific experience, but with God's help and
our praying friends at our church, I know Sophie is
going to be okay; maybe not today, but eventually.

CHAPTER 43
Sophie

"Jeremy? Are you still here?" I asked since I was surrounded by a curtain at the hospital.

"You bet I'm here, Sophie. I'm not going anywhere. Can I come in there or are they still examining you?"

"You can come in." As he opens the curtain, I open my arms again for a hug from my stepbrother, my hero.

"I keep thinking I'm going to run out of tears, I've cried so many of them!" Sophie said as she let go of Jeremy.

"Me too, Sophie. I'm so thankful you are alive! How the heck did you know how to set up the obstacle course you did for Roy?! It was unbelievably awesome!" Jeremy said with awe.

"Well, you taught me how to make a noose in high school, remember that play I was in? And I watched enough of those MacGyver series with Dad to know you have to use whatever you got and make it work to your advantage. I was so fortunate there was good stuff in the pool checkout room for me to use!"

"Roy Klindt messed with the wrong girl!" Jeremy said shaking his head.

"You bet he did, and he is going to live to regret it," I said nodding.

After answering a zillion questions at the hospital with Jeremy holding my hand throughout the entire process, I was finally released after being assigned to a therapist. I can't wait to get home and see my little sister and my mom.

"Soey!" my little sister yelled with delight as she ran to me with outstretched arms. I hugged her with all my might and remembered thinking a day or two ago I might never get to do this again. I close my eyes as tears squeeze out and run down my face. "Soey, cryin'?" Gretchen asked with her caring brown eyes.

"Yes, but happy crying, Gretchie," I said.

"Good! Good! Good! Soey! Missed you!" Gretchen said as she hugged my knees this time.

"And I missed you, too, little one."

CHAPTER 44
Amber

I've never been so thankful in my entire life. I'm so emotionally drained; I can hardly imagine what my poor Sophie endured those three days in captivity. She is a rock, but I know she is hurting right now; I can see it in her eyes. Sophie is clinging to Jeremy like a security blanket. I heard her tell him how she prayed almost non-stop those three days and was so thankful for what Jeremy taught her about the scripture, prayer and praising God with song. She said she did all of it and feels it is what kept her going.

Josh described the confinement and what Sophie had created inside the aquatic center check room. I smile as I say out loud to God, "She never gave up." Maybe at some point she can tell us the whole story, but for now bits and pieces are coming out when she is ready to let go of them. We can wait.

Bradley is coming shortly, and I thought Sophie would be anticipating his arrival, but she seems the total opposite. I hope Bradley is patient with So-phie. She needs lots of patience and understanding right now.

I open the door and say, "Come in Bradley! It's good to see you again! Sophie is in her bedroom upstairs. You can go on up."

"Thanks, Amber, it's good to see you again, too."

Bradley is carrying a bouquet of tulips—Sophie's fa-vorite flower as he takes the stairs two at a time, just like old times. I send off a silent prayer, *Lord, I hope all goes well with Bradley and Sophie, but your will be done.*

CHAPTER 45
Josh

"Amber? I need to tell you something. I should have told you a long time ago—I just thought I could handle it, but I found out that I can't.

"What is it, Josh?" Amber asked with a worried expression.

"I've got a gambling problem and it's been going on for years. I can't even tell you the thousands of dollars I've lost to this stupid habit. It's obscene. And it's why I was not able to buy Sophie a used vehicle when she left for college, because I gambled it away. I'm so very sorry."

Amber was speechless for a full minute and finally replied, "Josh? Are you going to do it again? Gamble I mean?"

"No, never. The idea of it used to be thrilling to me and now I just feel sick to my stomach even thinking of gambling. I'm DONE with it. With you and God as my witness, I will never EVER gamble again. I don't know if I can ever forgive myself what I put Sophie through because I spent the money we had saved for her car on gambling, but I found a *Gamblers Anonymous* group that meets on Monday nights in Ames, and I plan to start attending."

Amber said, "I believe you, Josh, and I believe IN you. I know you've got this. I forgive you and I know God forgives you. Now YOU need to forgive yourself. There is nothing to say this may have still happened whether or not you had purchased a car for Sophie, so don't go blaming yourself for everything. Lots of kids go to college without a vehicle and most of the time they don't need one. The important thing is we have our Sophie back; we didn't lose her!"

"I know," I say as I choke up and can barely talk. "We need to thank all our church prayer warriors tomorrow at church. When Sophie feels better, maybe we can have a cookout or something over here for all our church friends."

"I love that idea, Josh! I know all their prayers helped us get through this horrible ordeal. But it's not over yet for Sophie. She is going to need all of us that love her to keep praying and keep listening and support her. This was a harrowing experience for her and one she won't likely be able to let go of for a while. But I do love your idea of a cookout sometime in the future!"

Nodding, I said, "Did I see Bradley drive up a little

while ago?"

"Yes, he is upstairs with Sophie. I don't know how that will go, but if it is meant to be, God will give Bradley the patience to weather through this with Sophie."

CHAPTER 46
Sophie

"Knock, knock, it's me, Soph."

"Come in, Bradley," I say as I reach out to him for a hug. He kisses me passionately, but I feel nothing. I need to tell him, but he will be devastated.

"I'm so glad you are okay, Soph! I was so worried about you! I don't know what I would have done if something had happened to you!" Bradley said as he hugged me again.

My eyes are leaking again as I hug Bradley, unable to speak because I am choking up and thinking, but *something DID happen to me, Bradley.*

Bradley said, "I thought we could announce our engagement a little earlier than Christmas since we are all here! What do you think? And have you looked into transferring your classes to UNI yet?"

I sighed taking my time before answering, "Bradley, I need some time and I need to tell you what happened to me. We agreed to save ourselves for each other and I can't do that now. I can't marry you any time soon. I'm so sorry, but I just need to heal up and get ME okay right now and not worry about anything or anyone else."

"Well, we can just get engaged then and play it by ear when we decide to get married. People will understand," Bradley said as he held my hands. "And I don't want to hear what happened to you. Let's just forget it happened. You couldn't help it and that's all I need to know. I'd rather not hear what he did to you."

"No, Bradley, I can't get engaged to you right now either. I just can't. With what is going on inside me right now, I just can't; it wouldn't be right or fair to you. I've got a lot of stuff I need to work through, and I have a feeling it is going to take a while. I've decided I'm going to take at least the next semester off from college and just live here at home with my family. Dad is going to go get my stuff at ISU next week and bring it home."

"What are you saying, Sophie? You don't want to marry me anymore?"

I slowly shake my head and say, "No, Bradley, I'm so sorry, but I just can't make that commitment right now."

"EVER?" Bradley asks with confusion.

"All I know is how I feel right now, and I feel dead inside, devoid of any feelings for you. I can't promise you that I'll get over this and be okay. I might never be okay again and want to marry you. I'm sorry, Bradley. I need to return your ring to you," I said as I slipped it into his hand.

Bradley dropped his head and nodded, opening my bedroom door and leaving. I heard him rush down the stairs, and out our front door and tear out of our driveway with his vehicle. I sat down and just sobbed. This was the hardest thing I have ever done. I hated hurting Bradley, but I had to be honest.

My mom came into my room shortly after Bradley's sudden departure and saw me crumpled in a corner and just hugged me tight, not saying a word.

I started my therapy sessions the following week and liked my Christian therapist. I could talk openly to her and not feel judged. I told her about the safe place God allowed me to go to whenever Roy was on top of me, and she said it was quite common. She explained it in a way that made so much sense to me. She said God wouldn't allow Roy to take your mind and soul, so He gave you an avenue to travel elsewhere to a place you felt safe and secure so that Roy couldn't harm that piece of you. I liked that. I told the therapist I tried to stay in my safe place afterwards, but God wouldn't let me. She explained that in saying that maybe He wanted you to be able to think and figure out how to get out of the situation and you DID! You couldn't have done that if you had stayed in your safe place continually.

I'm still a mess, but I'm working through stuff; stuff that I still find confusing. My therapist asked me why I let Bradley go and I told her that I just couldn't worry about getting better for him and I didn't want to have to worry about the relationship. I just wanted to concentrate on myself. Bradley didn't seem to understand any of it and thought we could just pick right up where we left off before the abduction. I told my therapist I literally had no feelings for Bradley. I don't know where they went or what happened to them, they are just gone. I'm blaming them on my abduction, but she seems to think it could be something else. Anyway, I'm getting better little by little, day by day.

Dad tells me Jordan is doing better at school. He's been picking up some my stuff in the dorm room every Monday when he goes down for his *Gambling Anonymous* sessions. I was so surprised to hear him say that he had a problem with gambling. I would never have guessed that in a million years. Jordan told Dad to tell me "Hi" and gave him a handwritten note to give me. It sounds like she has cleaned up her act and ended the semester with a 1.9 GPA. She said she feels confident she can get that up to a 2.0 GPA by next semester. She is still attending tutoring sessions, this semester in geometry. I'm glad for her and glad she has made some progress in her life.

Jordan also apologized for bringing Roy into our lives, but I don't blame her for that.

It turns out that Roy admitted he killed his mom and buried her in their backyard. He told the authorities of the numerous graves where he had tortured and killed various animals over the years and then admitted to killing Cynthia Coate, the Ames lifeguard back in September. So sad to think about that girl enduring what I did only much, much longer. She must have felt so hopeless; I know I sure did at some point.

My stepbrother, Jeremy, stops over every weekend to see us and we have spent many hours talking on the phone as well. He is the best. He doesn't push me. He just listens patiently. He totally gets me and always has. I don't know what I'd do without Jeremy in my life.

One of my friends from high school attends UNI and saw Bradley with a girl last week on campus. It's interesting that I don't feel any jealousy, any regret hearing this, nothing. That's not to say my feelings might change in the future, but I just couldn't promise that to Bradley and he, evidently, couldn't wait it out. But I understand. Everyone needs to get on with their lives and I do, too. And I am. Day by day.

It's been several months now since my abduction, and I am starting to get my mojo back. My advisor from ISU sent me an email and told me that she was talking to a friend of hers that worked for the City of Ames. They are looking for an events co-ordinator. Her friend had heard about my success with the blood drive (through my advisor, I'm sure!) and wondered if she could contact me about a job opening at the City. My advisor wanted to see how I was doing and whether she could give her friend my email address. She told me I would be perfect for the job and added she told her friend that as well.

I didn't answer my advisor right away. I thought about it for a few days and prayed about it. I talked to Jeremy and my parents about it and finally I emailed my advisor back and said, "Yes, please. I think I'm ready."

I sent the City my resume, was interviewed by phone and I got the job! I'm able to work from home for another six weeks and when the fall term starts, the City of Ames wants me in the office. The events coordinator job will be 30 hours a week and the best part is that the City is paying for my college classes going forward while I am working for them!

I was telling my therapist my good news and she asked me a few questions like where I'm going to live and what I am feeling. I told her Jeremy had invited me to live with him off campus in his apart-ment since he never did find a roommate and my dad found me a good used car to take back to school and drive back and forth to my job and apartment.

I told her I felt everything had just fallen into place for me. She then asked me about my feelings for Jeremy and I told her I loved him—he's my brother. She asked me to go home and think about what I love about Jeremy and to examine my feelings— that is my assignment for next week.

I filled out page after page of why I love Jeremy and his positive, wonderful traits; it was easy! I found myself smiling the whole time I was writing each of Jeremy's traits filling out three pages and the backsides, too. I sat cross-legged on my bedroom floor and realized...I not only LOVE Jeremy, I think I might be IN love with Jeremy! But wait, should I shut that down? Is it wrong to love my stepbrother THAT way? I never let myself go there in the past since Bradley was my boyfriend, but Jeremy and I aren't related by blood so it's okay, right? I can't believe I had not figured this out earlier. But is Jeremy IN love with me, that's the question. And if he is not, I need to accept that, because I need Jeremy in my life even if it is just as a stepbrother.

CHAPTER 47
Jeremy

I'm excited for Sophie and her new job and can hardly wait for her to move into my two-bedroom apartment with me! It's a good sign she is mending and wanting to get back to living life again. I've been praying for her every single day. She is so precious; I get tears in my eyes thinking about what she went through. When Sophie wants to talk about those three days, I listen, and we bawl our eyes out together holding each other tight. She is so strong. I thank God for her in my life.

I'm headed to Fort Dodge today for the weekend to spend it with Sophie and her family. I'm hoping to take some of Sophie's things back to my apartment, so she won't have so much to move down the road.

Amber told me she is making potato salad and Josh is grilling tonight for supper. I can hardly wait for Amber's home cooking! Sophie meets me at my car and helps me carry in my laptop while I carry in my overnight bag. Something is different about So-

176

phie…I can't quite put my finger on it, though.

"Jeremy? Can we talk upstairs?" Sophie asked me.

"Sure, Sophie," I said, as I untangled myself from little Gretchen who was attached to my ankle holding tight as I walked to the stairs.

Sophie told me about her assignment for the week that her therapist appointed her. I sat there smiling while she read aloud the three pages—front and back--of traits she loves about me. When Sophie was done, she looked up at me with tears in her eyes.

I hugged her tight and said, "Sophie, all those traits are YOU as well in MY book! I love you, too, Sophie!"

"But are you IN love with me, Jeremy? Because I think I am IN love with you," Sophie said with tears falling into her lap.

I looked up at the ceiling of Sophie's room and said, "Thank you, God! I have loved you, Sophie and been IN love with you for a <u>very</u> <u>long</u> <u>time</u>. I'm SO very thankful you feel the same way!"

We hugged and laughed and kissed and repeated for nearly five minutes. Then we ran downstairs and told Amber and Josh. And get this: THEY ALREADY KNEW IT!

***

ACKNOWLEDGEMENTS

I would like to thank my biggest cheerleader and best buddy, Mary (Petey) Smith who walked and talked with me throughout the process of writing my first and second book. She was a constant encourager telling me I could do it and believed in me every step of the way. She was my sounding board and inspiration, giving me ideas as well as letting me bounce ideas off her. Next, I would like to thank my daughter Stacy, the grammar police and editor, for her wonderful help in perusing my fiction novels and cheering me on. Finally, I would like to thank my husband, Kim, for his patience in my writing and my daughter, Sara, for her timely encouragement. Thanks for reading my fiction novel. I enjoyed writing every single chapter. I hope you enjoyed reading it.

Made in the USA
Coppell, TX
30 April 2022

77260051R00105